A Tragedy By the Sea
and Other Stories

BY

HONORE DE BALZAC

J. H. SEARS & COMPANY, INC.
PUBLISHERS
NEW YORK

Set up, Printed and Bound at the
KINGSPORT PRESS
KINGSPORT TENNESSEE
United States of America

CONTENTS

A TRAGEDY BY THE SEA

THE path leading from Le Croisic to Batz town was not a beaten way; a puff of wind was enough to efface every trace left by the cart-wheels or the print of the horses' hoofs. However, our guide's practiced eye was able to discover it by the track of cattle and sheep dung. This path in some places went down to the sea, and in others rose toward the fields, according to the lay of the land, and the position of the rocks which it skirted.

It was noon, and we had only gone half way.

"We can rest over there," I said, pointing to a headland composed of lofty rocks. It looked as if we might find a nook there.

When the fisherman, whose eyes followed the direction of my finger, heard this, he shook his head, and said: "There is some one there. Every one who goes from Batz town to Le Croisic, or from Le Croisic to Batz town, always goes round another way, so as not to pass him."

The man murmured these words in a low tone that suggested mystery.

"Is it a robber then, or a murderer?"

Our guide's only answer was a deep, hollow exclamation, which redoubled our curiosity.

3

"But if we do go by, will anything happen to us?"

"Oh! no."

"Will you go by with us?"

"No, Monsieur."

"Well, we will go, if you can assure us that there is no danger."

"I could not say that," answered the fisherman quickly. "I only know that he who is there will not say anything to you, and will do you no harm. Good God! only he won't stir an inch from where he sits."

"What is he then?"

"A man!"

I never heard two syllables uttered in such a tragic tone. At that moment we were about twenty paces from a creek in which the sea was tossing. Our guide took the road which skirted the rocks; we went on straight in front of us, but Pauline took my arm. Our guide hastened his steps, in order to reach the place where the two paths met at the same time that we did. He evidently divined that after we had seen the man we should walk on quickly. This circumstance inflamed our curiosity, which then became so burning that our hearts beat as if we had been struck by a feeling of terror.

In spite of the heat of the day, and a sort of fatigue caused by our walk through the sands, our souls were still filled with the indescribable languor of intense delight. They were full of pure pleasure that can only be expressed by comparing it to the pleasure one feels in listening to exquisite music, such music as the "Andiamo mio ben" of Mozart. The melting together of two hearts in one pure thought is like the blending of two beautiful voices in song.

To be able to appreciate fully the emotion that seized us afterward, you must have shared the half voluptuous delight into which our morning's ramble had plunged us. Sit for a while and watch a wood-dove, with all its beautiful shades of color, perched on a branch that sways above a rivulet, and you will cry aloud with grief when you see it struck to the heart by the iron claws of a hawk and borne away with murderous speed, swift as powder drives a bullet from a gun.

We soon reached a small cave, in front of which was a narrow ledge, a hundred feet above the sea, protected from the fury of the waves by a sheer wall of rock. Before we had gone two steps on this platform, we felt an electric shiver run through us, not unlike the start one gives at a sudden noise in the middle of a still night.

We saw seated on a piece of rock a man who looked at us.

His glance darted from his bloodshot eyes like the flash of a cannon. The stoic stillness of his limbs I can only liken to the unchanging piles of granite amid which he sat. His whole body remained rigid, as if he had been turned into stone; only his eyes moved slowly. After casting upon us this look which had moved us so strongly, he withdrew his eyes and fixed them on the ocean stretched out at his feet. In spite of the light that streamed upward from it, he gazed upon it without lowering his eyelids, as the eagle is said to gaze upon the sun. He did not raise his eyes again. Try and recall, my dear uncle, one of those old butts of oak that time has stripped of all its branches, whose knotted trunk rears its fantastic form by the side of some lonely road; it will give you a true likeness of this man. His was the frame of Hercules in ruins, the face of Olympian Zeus wasted by age, and grief, and coarse food, and the hard life of them that toil on the sea; it was as it were charred by a thunderbolt. I looked at his hard and hairy hands, and I saw the sinews like bands of iron. In his whole frame were manifest signs of the same natural power.

In a corner of the little cave I noticed a great heap of moss, and a sort of rough shelf formed by chance in the face of the granite. On this shelf stood an earthen pitcher covered with the fragment of a round loaf. Never had my imagination—when it bore me into the deserts where the first Christian hermits dwelt —drawn a picture of grander religion or more terrible repentance. Even you, my dear uncle, who have experience of the Confessional, have never perhaps seen such noble remorse; here was remorse drowned in the waves of supplication,. the perpetual supplication of dumb despair.

This fisherman, this mariner, this rough Breton was sublime; I knew it, but I knew not why. Had those eyes wept? That hand, like the hand of a rough-hewn statue, had it struck? That rugged brow, stamped with fierce integrity, whereon strength had left the impress of the gentleness that is the heritage of all true strength—that brow, scarred deep with furrows, was it in harmony with a great heart? Why did the man sit there in granite? Why had the granite passed into the man? Which was humanity, which was stone?

A world of thought took possession of our brains. As our guide had anticipated, we passed on quickly in silence. When we met he must have seen that we were filled with horror and astonishment, but he did not confront us with the truth of his predictions; he only said—

"You have seen him?"

"What is the man?" said I.

"The people call him 'the man under a vow.'"

You can imagine the movement with which our heads turned toward the fisherman at these words! He was a simple man; he understood our mute interrogation, and this is what he told us. I try to preserve his own words and the popular character of the story.

"Madame, people at Le Croisic, and Batz too, believe that this man has been guilty of some crime and is performing the penance given him by a well-known rector whom he went to confess to beyond Nantes. Others believe that Cambremer—that is his name—is under a spell, and that he communicates it to any one who passes him to leeward. For this reason many people look to see in what quarter the wind is before they will pass the rock. If there's a gale," and he pointed to the northwest, "they would not go on, not if they were going to fetch a bit of the true cross; they are afraid and turn back. Others, the rich people at Le Croisic, say that Cambremer has made a vow, so he is called 'the man under a vow.' There he is night and day; he never goes. This talk has a smack of truth. Look," said he, turning round to point us out a thing we had not noticed before, "there, on the left, he has set up a wooden cross, to show that he is under the protection of God and the Blessed Virgin and the Saints. He would not be let alone as he is, if it were not that the terror he causes every one makes him as safe as if he were guarded by a regiment of soldiers. He has not spoken a word since he shut himself up, as it were, out there in the open. He lives upon bread and water which his brother's child, a little wench of twelve years old, takes him every morning. He has made a will and left her all his goods—a pretty creature she is too, a little slip of a maid, as gentle as a lamb, and as pretty spoken as could be. Her eyes are as blue—and as long as that," said he, holding up his thumb, "and her hair is like a cherub's. If you ask her, 'Tell me, Pérotte' (that's what we call Pierrette; she is dedicated to Saint Pierre. Cambremer's name is Pierre; he is her godfather)—'Tell me, Pérotte,' he went on, 'what does uncle say to thee?' she'll answer, 'He says nothing to me, never—nothing at all.' 'Well, and what does he do?' 'He kisses me on the fore-head, on Sundays.' 'Thou'rt not afraid, then?' 'Why!' she says, 'he is my godfather! He won't let any one else take him his food but me.'

"Pérotte declares that he smiles when she comes, but you might as well talk of a sunbeam in a sea-fog, for it's said he's as gloomy as storm."

"But," said I, "you are exciting our curiosity, not satisfying it. Do you know what it was that brought him to this? Was it grief? or repentance? or madness? or crime? is he——"

"Ah, Monsieur, scarcely any one but I and my father know the truth about it. My mother, who is now dead, was servant to the Justice to whom Cambremer told the whole story. The people at the port say that the priest to whom he made his confession only gave him absolution on that condition. My poor mother overheard Cambremer without intending to, because the Justice's parlor was next the kitchen. She heard it, and she is dead, and the judge who heard it, he too is dead. My mother made us promise—father and me—never to speak of it to the people about here; but I can tell you this: the evening my mother told us the story the hairs of my head stood on end."

"Well, tell us the story, my good fellow; we will not mention it to any one."

The fisherman looked at us and continued thus: "Pierre Cambremer, whom you saw there, is the eldest of the Cambremers. They have all been seafarers, fathers and sons, for generations. As their name shows, the sea has always given way to them. The one you have seen was a fisherman, with craft of his own; he had boats in which he used to go sardine fishing, and he even fished for deep sea fish for the dealers. He would have fitted out a ship and fished for cod, if he had not loved his wife so much. She was a beautiful woman, a Brouin from Guérande—splendid she was —and a kind heart too. She was so fond of her husband that she could never bear him to leave her longer than was necessary for the sardine fishing. Stop! They lived down there—there," said the fisherman, going up onto a mound, in order to point out an island in a sort of a little mediterranean between the dunes on which we were walking and the salt marshes of Guérande. "Do you see that house? That was his house. Jacquette Brouin and Cambremer had only one child, a boy, whom they loved—how much shall I say?—Dame! like an only child; they were quite mad about him. If their little Jacques had done something into their broth—excuse me, Madame—they'd have sworn it only made it all the sweeter. How often we used to see them at the fair buying him all the finest toys! It was a folly, every one told them so. Little Cambremer soon saw he could do anything he liked, and grew up as vicious as a red ass. If any one came to his father and said, 'Your son has almost killed little So-and-So!' he'd only laugh and say, 'Bah, he'll make a fine sailor! he'll command the king's fleet one day.' Or another would say, 'Pierre Cambremer, do you know that your lad has put out Pougaud's little girl's eye?' 'There'll be a lad for the girls!' said Pierre. Nothing was wrong with him. Then at ten years old the young whelp would fight every one he met; he'd wring the fowls' necks and gut the pigs for sport. I'll swear he wallowed in blood like a pole-cat! 'He'll make a splendid soldier,' said Cambremer; 'he has got a taste for blood.'

"You see, I remembered all this afterward," said the fisherman. "And so did Cambremer," he added, after a pause.

"By the time Jacques Cambremer was fifteen or sixteen he was—well! a perfect shark. He used to go and play the fool and kick up his heels at Guérande and Savenay. Next he wanted coin; so he set to robbing his mother, and she didn't dare to say a word of it to her husband. Cambremer was an honest man; if a man had given him two *sous* too much on a bill, he would go twenty leagues to return them.

"At last, one day his mother was plundered of everything while his father was away fishing; their son carried off the dresser, the crockery, the sheets, the linen; he left nothing but the four walls. He sold the whole of it to go on the spree with to Nantes. The poor woman cried over it for days and nights. His father would have to be told when he came back, and she was afraid of his father—not for herself—you may be sure! When Pierre Cambremer came back and saw his house furnished with things lent to his wife, he said, 'What in the world is all this?' His poor wife was more dead than alive. At last she said, 'We have been robbed.' 'And where is Jacques?' 'Jacques is away on the spree.' No one knew where the good-for-nothing fellow had gone. 'He's too fond of his larks,' said Pierre.

"Six months afterward the poor father heard that his son was going to be taken before the Justice at Nantes. He journeys there on foot (it's quicker than by sea), lays hands on his son, and brings him back. He doesn't ask him, 'What hast been doing?' He only says, 'If thou dost not stay here for two years with thy mother and me, and keep thyself straight, and go fishing and live like an honest man, thou'lt have me to deal with.' The mad fellow, counting on his parent's folly, goes and makes an ugly face at his father. Thereupon Pierre gives him a cuff on the side of his head that lays up Master Jacques for six months. Meanwhile the poor mother was pining away with grief.

"One night she was sleeping peacefully beside her husband when she hears a noise; she raises herself in bed, and gets a blow from a knife in her arm. She cries out; they fetch a light, and Pierre Cambremer sees that his wife is wounded. He believes it is a robber—as if there were any robbers in our parts! Why, you might carry ten thousand *francs* in gold from Le Croisic to Saint-Nazare under your arm, and no fear of any one even asking you what you'd got

there.   Pierre goes to look for Jacques, but he can't
find him anywhere.   The next morning the villain
actually had the face to come back and say that he
had been at Batz.   I ought to tell you that his mother
did not know where to hide her money; Cambremer
placed his with Monsieur Dupolet at Croisic.   Their
son's pranks had cost them pounds upon pounds; they
were half ruined; it was a hard thing for people who
had about twelve thousand *livres* altogether, counting their little island.   No one knows how much Cambremer had to give at Nantes to get his son off.   The
whole family was in bad luck.   Cambremer's brother
had met with misfortunes and wanted help.   To console him Pierre told him that Jacques should marry
Pérotte (the younger Cambremer's child).   Then, to
help him to gain a living he employed him at his fishing, for Joseph Cambremer was reduced to work for
his bread.   His wife had died of fever, so he had to
pay for the months of Pérotte's weaning.   Pierre Cambremer's wife too owed as much as a hundred *francs* to
different people, for the little one, for linen and clothes,
and for two or three months' wages to big Frelu, who
had a child by Simon Gaudry, and nursed Pérotte.
Well, Cambremer's wife had sewn a Spanish coin into
the wool of her mattress, with 'For Pérotte' written
on it.   She had had a fine education, and could write
like a clerk; she had taught her son to read; it was that
was the ruin of him.   No one knows how it was, but
that good-for-nothing Jacques had sniffed gold; he had
taken it and gone to run riot at Le Croisic.   The good
man Cambremer—as ill-luck would have it—came
home with his boat, and as he was landing he sees a
bit of paper floating on the water; he picks it up and

takes it to his wife; she recognizes the words in her own writing, and falls down on the floor. Cambremer says nothing, goes to Le Croisic, and hears there that his son is playing billiards; then he asks to see the woman that keeps the *café*, and says to her, 'Jacques will pay you with a certain gold piece which I told him not to pay away; if you will return it to me I will wait at the door and give you silver for it instead.' The good woman brought him the coin. Cambremer takes it. 'Good,' says he, and returns home. The whole town knew that much. But this is what I know, and the rest can only just guess at. He tells his wife to set their downstair room in order; he makes a fire in the grate, lights two dips, and sets two chairs on one side of the hearth and a stool on the other. Then he tells his wife to lay out his wedding clothes, and bids her rig herself out in hers. He puts on his clothes, and when he is dressed he goes for his brother and tells him to keep watch outside the house, and warn him if he hears any sound on either of the two beaches—this one and the one by the marsh de Guérande. When he thinks his wife has dressed herself, he goes in again, loads his gun, and hides it in the chimney-corner. Presently Jacques comes home; he is late; he had been drinking and gambling up till ten o'clock; he had got brought across at Carnouf Point. His uncle hears him shouting on the beach by the marshes and goes to fetch him, and brings him over without saying anything. When he comes in, his father points to the stool and says, 'Sit thee down there. Thou art before thy father and mother whom thou hast offended; they must be thy judges.' Jacques began to howl, because Cambremer's face had a strange, set look. His mother

sat as stiff as an oar. 'If thou dost cry or budge an
inch, if thou dost not sit there as straight as a mast on
thy stool,' said Pierre, taking aim at his son with his
gun, 'I'll kill thee like a dog.' The son became as
dumb as a fish; the mother said no word. 'Look here,'
said Pierre to his son; 'here is a piece of paper which
has been used to wrap up a Spanish gold piece in; the
gold piece was in thy mother's bed; thy mother was the
only person who knew where she put it; I found the
paper floating on the water when I landed; thou hast
just given—this very evening—this Spanish gold piece
to la mère Fleurant, and thy mother cannot find her
piece in the bed. Explain.' Jacques said that he had
not taken his mother's piece, and that his piece he had
by him, left over from Nantes. 'So much the better,'
said Pierre. 'How canst thou prove that to us?' 'I
had it.' 'Thou didst not take thy mother's?' 'No.'
'Canst thou swear it on thy eternal salvation?' He
was going to swear; his mother raised her eyes and
looked at him and said, 'Jacques, my child, take care;
do not swear what is not true; thou canst amend, and
repent; there is still time.' She wept. 'You're a nice
one,' said he; 'you have always tried to get me into
scrapes.' Cambremer turned pale. 'What thou hast
just said to thy mother will make thy account all the
heavier. Let's come to the point! Art going to
swear?' 'Yes.' 'Wait a minute,' said he. 'Had thy
coin got this cross on it that the sardine merchant put
on ours when he gave it us?' Jacques was getting
sober; he began to cry.—'We've talked enough,' said
Pierre; 'I am not going to say anything about what
thou hast done before, but I don't choose that a Cambremer should die in the Market-place at Le Croisic.

Say thy prayers, and let's make haste. There's a priest
coming in a minute to hear thy confession.' His
mother had gone out; she could not stay to hear her
son condemned. When she was gone, Cambremer
the uncle, came with the Rector of Piriac; but Jacques
would have nothing to say to him. He was a cunning
one; he knew his father well enough to be sure he
would not kill him without confession. 'Thank you,
Monsieur,' said Cambremer, seeing that Jacques was
obstinate; 'please to excuse us, but I wanted to give my
son a lesson; I beg you not to say anything about it.
As to thee,' he said to Jacques, 'if thou dost not mind
—the first time it'll be for good and all. I shall put
an end to it without confession.' He sent him to bed.
The lad believed this, and imagined that he would be
able to set himself to rights with his father. He slept;
the father watched. When he saw that his son was in a
deep sleep, he covered his mouth with tow, bound it
round tightly with a piece of sail, and then tied his
hands and feet. He raved, 'he wept blood,' as Cambremer told the Justice. You may imagine, his mother
threw herself at his father's feet. 'He is judged,'
said he; 'thou must help me to put him into the boat.'
She refused. Cambremer put him in by himself,
forced him down into the bottom of the boat, and tied
a stone to his neck. Then he rowed out of the cove—
out to the open sea till he was as far out as the rock
where he now sits. By that time the poor mother had
got her brother-in-law to take her out there. She cried
out as loud as she could, 'Mercy,' but it was only like
throwing a stone at a wolf. It was moonlight; she
. saw the father throw their son, to whom her bowels
still yearned, into the sea; and as there was no wind

she heard Plsh! then nothing, not a trace, not a bubble. No, the sea doesn't tell secrets. Cambremer landed to quiet his wife's groans, and found her half dead. It was impossible for the two brothers to carry her; they were obliged to put her in the boat which had just been used for her son, and rowed her round by the Le Croisic channel. Ah, well! *la belle Brouin,* as she was called, did not last a week; she died entreating her husband to burn the cursed boat. Oh! he did it too. As for him, it was all up with him; he didn't know what he wanted. When he walked, he staggered like a man who can't stand wine. Then he took a ten days' journey, and when he came back, sat down where you have seen him, and since he has been there he hasn't spoken a word."

.   .   .   .   .

The fisherman did not take more than a minute or two to tell us this story, and told it even more simply than I have written it. The people make few reflections when they tell a tale; they relate the fact that has impressed them, and only translate it into words as they feel it. This narrative was as keen and incisive as the blow of a hatchet.

"I will not go to Batz," said Pauline, when we reached the upper side of the lake.

We returned to Le Croisic by the salt marshes. Our fisherman, become as silent as ourselves, led us through the bewildering paths. Our souls had undergone a change. We were both plunged in gloomy thoughts, saddened by this drama which explained the sudden presentiment we had felt at the sight of Cambremer. We both knew enough of the world to divine that part of those three lives concerning which our guide

had been silent. The miseries of the three rose up before us as plainly as if we had seen them in scenes of a
drama that reached its climax in the father's expiation
of his necessary crime. We dared not look at the
rock where the unhappy man sat, a terror to the whole
country. Clouds began to darken the sky, and a mist
rose on the horizon while we walked through the most
gloomy and melancholy scenery I ever beheld. We
trod on soil that seemed sick and unwholesome, the
salt marshes, that may well be called the scrofulous
places of the earth. The ground is divided into un-
equal squares, each encased in a deep cutting of gray
earth, and each full of brackish water, on the surface
of which the salt collects. These artificial pits are
divided within by borders, whereon the workmen walk
armed with long rakes. By the aid of these rakes they
skim off the brine and carry it to round platforms contrived at certain distances, when it is ready to be
formed into heaps. For two hours we walked by
the side of this gloomy chessboard, where the abun-
dance of salt chokes all vegetation, and where no one
is to be seen, except here and there a few *paludiers*—
the name given to the cultivators of the salt. These
men, or rather this class of Bretons, wear a special
dress, a white jacket, not unlike a brewer's. They
marry only among themselves; there is no instance of
a girl of this tribe having married any other man than a
paludier. The horrible appearance of these swamps,
with the mud thus raked in regular patches, and
the gray earth shunned by every Breton flower,
was in harmony with the pall that had been cast upon
our souls. When we reached the place where one has
to cross the arm of the sea formed by the irruption of

its waters into this basin and no doubt serving to re-
plenish the salt marshes, the sight of even such meager
vegetation as adorns the sands on the beach was a delight to us. As we were crossing, we could see in the
middle of the lake the island on which the Cambremers
had lived. We turned away our heads.

On arriving at our hotel, we noticed a billiard table
in one of the ground-floor rooms, and when we learned
that it was the only public billiard table in Le Croisic,
we made our preparations for leaving during the night.
The next day we were at Guérande.

DON JUAN;
OR THE ELIXIR OF LONG LIFE

DON JUAN; OR THE ELIXIR OF LONG LIFE

ON a winter's night, in a sumptuous palace at Ferrara, Don Juan Belvidero was entertaining a Prince of the house of Este. At this period a banquet was a wonderful scene, possible only for the riches of royalty and the power of Princes.

Round a table lit with perfumed tapers sat seven joyous women bandying sweet talk. About them the noblest marble of the greatest masters gleamed white against walls of crimson stucco, and formed a contrast with the gorgeous colors of carpets brought from Turkey.

These women, clad in satin, glittering with gold, loaded with jewels only less brilliant than their eyes, told each her tale of overpowering passions, diverse as their own charms. But among them was no difference either of thought or expression; a movement, a look, a gesture supplied their words with commentaries wanton, lewd, melancholy, or scoffing.

One seemed to say: "My beauty can rekindle the ice-bound heart of age."

Another: "I love to lie couched among my cushions and think, drunk with the passion of those who adore me."

A third, a novice at such feasts, would fain have blushed. "In the depth of my heart," she said, "I feel remorse! I am a Catholic, and I fear hell. But I love you so much, so—so much that for you I can sacrifice eternity."

The fourth cried, as she drained a cup of Chian wine: "Joy, joy forever! Each morning dawns for me a new existence; each evening I drink deep of life, the life of happiness, the life of desire!"

The woman who sat by Belvidero looked at him with eyes of flame. She was silent. "I should not need a bravo to kill my lover if he deserted me!" She laughed; but her hand crushed convulsively a comfit box of wonderful workmanship.

"When shall you be Grand Duke?" asked a sixth of the Prince, an expression of murderous pleasure in her teeth, of bacchic delirium in her eyes.

"And you, when will your father be dead?" said the seventh, throwing her bouquet at Don Juan with a gesture of maddening playfulness. She was a girl, young and innocent, wont to laugh at all things sacred.

"Ah! do not speak of it," cried the young and handsome Juan Belvidero. "There is only one eternal father in the world, and as ill-luck will have it, he is mine."

The seven courtesans of Ferrara, the friends of Don Juan, and even the Prince himself, cried out with horror. Two hundred years later, under Louis XV., the most cultivated society would have laughed at this sally, but perhaps also, at the beginning of an orgy, the soul still sees with clearer eyes. In spite of the flame of candles, the fume of wines, the sight of gold and silver vessels; in spite of the cry of passion and the presence of women most ravishing to look upon, perchance there still brooded in the depths of their hearts a little of that reverence for human and divine things which still struggles on, until it is drowned by debauchery in the last sparkling waves of wine. Nevertheless, their flowers were already faded, their eyes already clouded, and drunkenness possessed them, after the saying of Rabelais, "Down to the heels of their boots." During a moment of silence a door opened, and, as at the feast of Belshazzar, God revealed Himself. He appeared under the form of an old servant, with white hair and wrinkled brow, and tottering footsteps. He entered with an air of sadness, and withered with one look the garlands, and the bowls of golden plate, and the pyramids of fruit, and all the brightness of the banquet, and the flush on the scared faces of the banqueters, and the colors of the cushions pressed by the white arms of the women; lastly, he cast a pall upon their revelry when with hollow voice he murmured these solemn words, "Sire, your father is dying." Don Juan rose, making a sign to his guests which might have been interpreted thus, "Excuse me, but this is not a thing which happens every day."

Does not a father's death often startle a young man in the midst of the splendors of life, in the very lap of frenzied debauchery? Death is as sudden in his whims as is a courtesan, but he is truer—he has never deceived any man.

When the door of the hall was shut, and Don Juan was passing through a long, gloomy gallery, where the cold was as great as the gloom, he bethought him of his part as a son, and strove to wear a mask to fit the filial character; for his mirth he had thrown aside with his napkin. The night was black. The silent servant who led the young man to the chamber of death lighted the way so dimly that Death was able, by the help of the cold, and the silence, and the gloom—and perhaps too of a recoil from drunkenness—to insinuate certain reflections into the mind of the reveller. He examined his life and grew thoughtful, as a man at law with another, on his way to the court.

Bartolomeo Belvidero, the father of Don Juan, was an old man of ninety years, who had spent almost all his life in the mazes of commerce. Having often travelled over the magic countries of the East, he had there acquired immense riches, and knowledge more precious, he said, than gold or diamonds; indeed for these he now cared scarcely at all. "I prefer a tooth to a ruby, and power to knowledge," he sometimes cried, and smiled as he spoke. This kind father loved to hear Don Juan relate his youthful frolics, and would say jestingly, as he lavished his gold upon him, "My dear child, only commit such follies as will really amuse thee." He was the only old man who has ever taken pleasure in the sight of another man's youth; his paternal love cheated his white hairs as he contemplated the brilliancy of this young life. At the age of sixty Belvidero became enamored of an angel of peace and beauty; Don Juan was the only fruit of this late and short-lived love. Now for fifteen years the old man had deplored the loss of his dear Juana; it was to this affliction of his old age that his numerous servitors and his son attributed the strange habits which he had contracted. Shut up in the most incommodious wing of his palace, he very rarely left it, and Don Juan himself could not penetrate into his father's apartment without having first obtained his permission. If this voluntary anchorite walked in his own palace or through the streets of Ferrara, he seemed to be searching for something he had lost. He walked as though in a dream, with undecided steps, preoccupied, like a man at war with an idea or a memory.

While the young man gave the most sumptuous banquets and the palace rang with bursts of merriment—while horses champed their bits in the courtyard and pages quarreled over their dice on the steps—Bartolomeo ate seven ounces of bread a day and drank water. If he required a little game, it was only to give the bones to a black spaniel, which was his constant companion. He never complained of the noise; during his sickness, if the sound of the horn and the baying of dogs startled him while he slept, he would only say, "Ah! it is Don Juan returning!" So complacent and indulgent a father was never met with before; thus the young Belvidero, being wont to treat him without consideration, had all the faults of spoilt children. He lived with Bartolomeo as a capricious courtesan lives with an old lover; he gained indulgence for impertinences by a smile; he sold him his good humor, and only allowed his love. As Don Juan reconstructed in thought the picture of his youth, he perceived that it would be difficult to find the kindness of his father at fault. Feeling a sort of remorse arise in the depth of his heart at the moment he was passing through the gallery, he almost felt he could forgive his father for having lived so long; he returned to some sentiment of filial piety just as a robber turns to honesty when the enjoyment of a successfully stolen million becomes a possibility. The young man had soon passed through the cold and lofty halls which composed his father's apartment. After having ex-

perienced the effects of a damp, chill atmosphere, and
inhaled the dense air and the musty odor given out
by the ancient tapestries and dusty presses, he found
himself in the old man's chamber, before a bed of
sickness close to a fire almost extinct. A lamp, placed
upon a table of Gothic design, shed its light in fitful
gleams, now brightly, now faintly, upon the bed, and
thus displayed the old man's face under ever-varying
aspects. The cold whistled through the ill-fitting casements, and the snow-flakes made a sullen murmur as
they scourged the panes. This scene formed so striking
a contrast to the scene Don Juan had just left that he
could not restrain a shudder.

Then he grew cold, for as he approached the bed
an unwonted flood of light, blown by a gust of wind,
lit up the head of his father: the features were dis-
torted, the skin clung closely to the bones, its greenish
tint rendered still more horrible by the whiteness of
the pillow whereon the old man lay; the open, tooth-
less mouth was drawn with pain, and let slip between it
sighs whose dolorous depth was sustained by the echo-
ing howls of the tempest. In spite of these signs of
dissolution, there beamed from this head an incredible
character of power; a mighty spirit was at war with
Death. The eyes, hollowed by sickness, preserved a
strange steadfastness; it seemed as though Bartolomeo would have slain with his last look an enemy sitting at the foot of his bed. This look, fixed and frigid,
was the more frightful because the head remained as
immovable as a skull upon the physician's table. The
entire body indicated by the bedclothes showed that
the old man's limbs also lay as rigid as the head. The
whole was dead except the eyes. Moreover, the sounds

that issued from his mouth had something automatic in them.

Don Juan felt a certain shame at coming to his father's death-bed still wearing the bouquet of a harlot in his breast, and carrying thither the perfumes of a banquet and the odors of wine. "Thou art enjoying thyself," said the old man, when he saw it was his son. At this moment the clear, light voice of a singer, who held the banqueters spellbound, sustained by the harmony of the viol on which she accompanied herself, rose above the rattle of the hurricane, and rang even in this funereal chamber. Don Juan affected not to hear the answer thus brutally given in the affirmative to his father. "I blame thee not, my child," said Bartolomeo. The kindness of these words caused a pang to Don Juan; he could not forgive his father for the poignancy of his goodness.

"My father, think of the remorse I must feel," said he hypocritically.

"Poor Juanino," replied the dying man in a muffled voice, "I have always been so kind to thee that thou couldst not desire my death?"

"Oh," cried Don Juan, "if it were only possible for me to restore life to you by giving you up a part of my own!"

("One can always say that sort of thing," thought the reveller; it is as though I offered the world to my mistress.") He had scarcely conceived this thought when the old spaniel barked. The intelligence of this voice made Don Juan shudder; it seemed to him as if the dog had understood him.

"I knew well, my son, that I could count upon thee," cried the dying man. "I shall live. Thou shalt have

thy wish. I shall live without depriving thee of a
single one of the days allotted thee."

"He is delirious," said Don Juan to himself. Then
he added aloud: "Yes, my dearest father, you will
live, assuredly, as long as I live, for your image will
be always in my heart."

"I was not speaking of that sort of life," said the
old noble. He collected all his strength and sat up,
for he was troubled by one of those suspicions that
only rise from under the pillows of the dying. "Listen!
my son," he replied in a voice enfeebled by this last
effort; "I am no more ready to die than thou art ready
to give up thy falcons, and dogs, and horses, and wine,
and mistresses, and gold."

"I can well believe it," thought his son again, as he
knelt down by the bedside and kissed one of the corpse-
like hands of Bartolomeo. "But," he answered aloud,
"my father, my dear father, we must submit to the
will of God."

"God is I," muttered the old man.

"Blaspheme not," cried the reveller, when he saw
the look of menace which his father's features assumed. "I beseech you take care; you have received
Extreme Unction; I could never be comforted if I saw
you die in sin!"

"Listen to me, wilt thou?" cried the dying man, his
mouth drawn with anger.

Don Juan held his peace. A horrible silence reigned.
Across the dull whir of the snow the harmonies of
that ravishing voice and the viol still travelled, faint as
the dawn of day. The dying man smiled.

"Thou hast bidden singers, thou hast brought music
hither; I thank thee. A banquet! Women, young

and beautiful, with white skins and raven locks!—all
the pleasures of life! Bid them stay; I am about to
be born again."

"The delirium is at its height," thought Don Juan.

"I have discovered a means of bringing myself to
life again. Here! Look in the drawer in the table;
it opens by pressing a spring hidden under the griffon."

"I have found it, my father."

"Good! take out a little flask of rock crystal."

"It is here."

"I spent twenty years in . . ." At this moment
the old man felt his end approaching; he collected all
his strength and said, "As soon as I have given my
last breath, rub me entirely all over with that water,
and I shall come to life again."

"There is very little of it," answered the young
man.

Though Bartolomeo could no longer speak, he still
retained the faculties of sight and hearing; at these
words his head turned round toward Don Juan with
a sudden spasmodic start, his neck remained stretched
out like the neck of a marble statue condemned by the
thought of the sculptor always to look to one side, his
eyes were dilated and had acquired a hideous stare. He
was dead, dead as he lost his last, his only illusion. He
had sought a refuge in the heart of his son; he found
it a charnel-house more hollow than men are wont to
dig for their dead. Thus it was that his hair stood on
end with horror, the convulsion in his eyes still spoke.
It was a father rising in rage from his tomb to demand
vengeance at the hand of God upon his son!

"Hm! The old man is done for," said Don Juan.

In his hurry to hold up the mysterious crystal before the light of the lamp, like a drunkard consulting his bottle at the end of a meal, he had not seen the pallor fall upon his father's eyes. The dog gaped as he gazed alternately at the elixir and his dead master, while Don Juan glanced to and fro at his father and the phial. The lamp cast up its flickering flames, the silence was profound, the viol was dumb. Belvidero shivered; he thought he saw his father move. Terrified by the set expression of those accusing eyes, he closed them as he would have shut a shutter shaken by the wind on an autumn night. He stood erect, motionless, lost in a world of thoughts. All at once a sharp sound, like the cry of a rusty spring, broke the silence. Don Juan, startled, almost dropped the phial. Sweat colder than the steel of a dagger broke from every pore. A cock of painted wood rose on the top of a clock and crowed three times. It was one of those ingenious machines which the students of those days used, to wake them at a fixed hour for their studies. The dawn already glowed red through the casements. Don Juan had spent ten hours in meditation. The old clock was more faithful in its service than was he in his duty toward Bartolomeo. The mechanism was composed of wood, and pulleys, and cords, and wheels, while he had within him that mechanism peculiar to man which is called a heart. Not to run any risk of spilling the mysterious liquid, Don Juan, the sceptic, placed it again in the little drawer of the Gothic table. At this solemn moment he heard in the galleries a stifled commotion; there were confused voices, muffled laughter, light footsteps, the rustling of silk—in short, the din of a merry troop trying to compose themselves. The door opened, and the Prince, the friends of Don

Juan, the seven courtesans, and the singers appeared in the quaint disorder of dancers surprised by the light of morning, when the sun struggles with the paling flames of the candles. They were all come to offer the customary consolations to the young heir.

"Ho! ho! poor Don Juan; can he really have taken this death to heart?" said the Prince in La Brambilla's ear.

"Well, his father was very kind," she answered.

The nocturnal meditations of Don Juan, however, had imprinted so striking an expression upon his features that it imposed silence on the group. The men stood motionless. The women, whose lips were parched with wine and whose cheeks were stained with kisses, fell upon their knees and tried to pray. Don Juan could not help shivering at the sight; splendor, and mirth, and laughter, and song, and youth, and beauty, and power, the whole of life personified thus prostrate before the face of Death.

But in this adorable Italy debauchery and religion were then so closely coupled that there, religion was a debauch, and debauchery a religion! The Prince pressed Don Juan's hand with unction; then, all the faces having simultaneously assumed the same grimace, half sadness, half indifference, this phantasmagoria disappeared and left the hall empty. Verily, it was an image of life. As they descended the stairs the Prince said to La Rivabarella: "Who would have thought that Don Juan's impiety was all a sham? Yet it seems he did love his father!"

"Did you notice the black dog?" asked Brambilla.

"Well, he is immensely rich," remarked Bianca Cavatolino, smiling.

"What's that to me?" cried the proud Veronese, she who had crushed the comfit box.

"What's that to you?" cried the Duke. "With his crowns he is as much a prince as I am."

At first, swayed by a thousand thoughts, Don Juan wavered between several plans. After having taken count of the treasure amassed by his father, toward evening he returned to the mortuary chamber, his soul big with a hideous egoism. In the apartment he found all the servants of the house busy collecting the ornaments of the state bed, on which their late lord was to be exposed on the morrow, in the midst of a superbly illuminated chapel; a grand sight which the whole of Ferrara would come to gaze at; Don Juan made a sign and his servants stopped, trembling and discomfited.

"Leave me here, alone," said he in an altered voice; "you need not return until I have gone."

When the steps of the old serving man, who was the last to go out, only sounded very faintly on the flagstones, Don Juan barred the door precipitately; then, certain that he was alone, he cried out: "Let us try!" The corpse of Don Belvidero was laid on a long table. In order to hide from every eye the hideous spectacle of a corpse of such extreme decrepitude and leanness that it was almost a skeleton, the embalmers had placed a cloth over it, which enveloped it entirely, with the exception of the head. This sort of mummy lay in the middle of the room; the cloth, naturally flexible, indicated vaguely the gaunt, stiff, sharp form of the limbs. The face was already marked with large livid stains, showing the necessity of finishing the embalming. In spite of his armor of scepticism, Don

Juan trembled as he took out the stopper of the magic crystal phial. When he had come up close to the head, he was compelled to wait a moment, he shivered so. But this young man had been early and skilfully corrupted by the manners of a dissolute court; an idea worthy of the Duke of Urbino gave him courage, and a feeling of keen curiosity spurred him on; it even seemed as if the fiend had whispered the words which re-echoed in his heart: "Anoint one eye!" He took a cloth, moistened it sparingly with the precious fluid, and rubbed it gently over the right eyelid of the corpse. The eye opened.

"Ah! ah!" exclaimed Don Juan, pressing the phial in his hands as in a dream we cling to a branch by which we hang over a precipice.

He saw an eye full of life, the eye of a child in the head of a corpse; in it the light quivered as though in the depth of a limpid pool; protected by the beautiful black lashes, it sparkled like those strange lights that the traveller sees in a desert country upon a winter's night.

This eye of fire seemed eager to start out upon Don Juan; it thought, accused, judged, condemned, menaced, spoke; it cried aloud, it bit. Every human passion pulsated in it; the tenderest supplication, a kingly wrath, the love of a maiden entreating her tormentors, the searching look on his fellows of the man who treads the last step to the scaffold. So much of life beamed in this fragment of life that Don Juan drew back in terror. He walked up and down the room; he dared not look upon this eye, yet he saw it on the floor, in the tapestries. The room was strewn with spots full of fire, and life, and intelligence.

Everywhere gleamed those eyes; they seemed to bay at his heels!

"He would certainly have lived another hundred years," he cried involuntarily, at the moment when, brought back by some diabolic influence to his father's side, he found himself gazing at this luminous spark.

All at once the intelligent eyelid shut and opened again hastily; it was like the look of a woman who gives consent. If a voice had cried out, "Yes!" Don Juan could not have been more terrified.

"What am I to do?" thought he. He had the courage to try and close the pallid eyelid, but his efforts were useless.

"Tear it out? That might be parricide, perhaps," he pondered.

"Yes," said the eye, quivering with astounding irony.

"Ha! ha!" cried Don Juan, "there is sorcery in it."

And he drew near to tear out the eye. A large tear rolled down the hollow cheeks of the corpse, and fell on Belvidero's hand.

"It burns," he cried, as he wiped it off.

This struggle was as tiring as if, like Jacob, he had been wrestling with an angel.

At last he rose, saying to himself, "If only there is no blood!"

Then summoning up all the courage necessary to be a coward, he tore out the eye, and crushed it in a cloth; he did not dare to look at it.

He heard a sudden, terrible groan. The old spaniel expired with a howl.

"Could it have been in the secret?" thought Don Juan, looking at the faithful animal.

Don Juan passed for a dutiful son. He erected a monument of white marble over his father's tomb, and entrusted the execution of the figures to the most celebrated artists of the time. He did not feel perfectly at his ease until the day when the statue of his father, kneeling before Religion, lay, an enormous pile, over his grave. In its depth was buried the only remorse which had ever, in moments of physical weariness, touched the surface of his heart. As he reviewed the immense riches amassed by the aged orientalist, Don Juan grew careful; had not the power of wealth gained for him two human lives? His sight penetrated to the depth and scrutinized the elements of social life, embracing the world the more completely in his gaze, because he looked upon it from the other side of the tomb.

He analyzed men and things only to have finished, once and forever, with the Past, shown forth by History; with the Present, represented by Law; with the Future, revealed by Religion. He took matter and the soul, he cast them into the crucible, and found—Nothing. From thenceforth he became DON JUAN!

Young and handsome, master of the illusions of life, he flung himself into it, despising yet possessing himself of the world. His happiness could not consist in that bourgeois felicity which is nourished on an occasional sop, the treat of a warming-pan in the winter, a lamp at night, and new slippers every three months. No; he seized on existence as an ape snatches a nut, but without amusing himself for long with the common husk, he skilfully stripped it off, in order to discuss the sweet and luscious kernel within. The poetry and the sublime transports of human passion did not seem worth a rap to him.

He was ever guilty of the fault of men of power who sometimes imagine that little souls believe in great ones, and so think to exchange high thoughts of the future for the small change of our transient notions. He was quite able to walk as they do, with his feet on the earth, and his head in the skies; but he preferred to sit down and parch under his kisses the fresh, tender, perfumed lips of many women; for, like Death, wherever he passed he devoured all without shame, desiring a love of full possession, oriental, of pleasures lasting long and gladly given. In women he loved not themselves, but woman. He made irony the natural habit of his soul. When his mistresses used their couch as a step whereby to climb into the heavens and lose themselves in the lap of intoxication and ecstasy, Don Juan followed them, as grave, sympathetic, and sincere as any German student. But he said I, while his mistress, lost in her delight, said we! He knew perfectly the art of being beguiled by a woman. He was always strong enough to make her believe that he trembled like a schoolboy at a ball, when he says to his first partner, "Do you like dancing?" But he could storm too, on occasion, and draw his sword to some purpose; he had vanquished great captains. There was raillery in his simplicity, and laughter in his tears—for he could shed tears at any moment—like a woman, when she says to her husband, "Give me a carriage, for I know I shall go into a consumption." To merchants the world is a bale or a heap of bills of exchange; for most young men it is a woman: for some women it is a man; for certain minds it is a drawing-

room, a clique, a district, a town; for Don Juan the
whole universe was himself. A model of grace and
high breeding, with all the charm of wit, he moored
his bark to every bank, but when he took a pilot on
board he only went whither he chose to be steered.

The longer he lived the more he doubted. By studying men, he discovered that courage is often rashness;
prudence, poltroonery; generosity, diplomacy; justice,
iniquity; scrupulousness, stupidity; honor, a convention; and by a strange fatality he perceived that those
who are truly honorable, of fine feeling, just, generous,
prudent, and courageous, gain no consideration among
men—"What a heartless jest!" thought he; "it cannot
be made by a God." So he renounced a better world,
never doffed his hat at the sound of a name, and
looked upon the stone saints in the churches as works
of art. But comprehending the organization of human
societies, he never did too much to offend their preju-
dices, because he knew that he was not so powerful
as their executioner. He deflected their laws with that
grace and *esprit* so well described in his scene with
Monsieur Dimanche; in fact, he was the type of *Don
Juan* of Molière, of the *Faust* of Goethe, of the *Man-
fred* of Byron, and of the *Melmoth* of Maturin, grand
figures drawn by the greatest geniuses of Europe, to
which the lyre of Rossini will some day perhaps be
wanting, no less than the harmonies of Mozart. Terrible images, perpetuated by the principle of evil ever
existent in man, images of which copies are found in
every age; whether the type enters into treaty with
man and becomes incarnate in Mirabeau; whether it is
content to work in silence like Bonaparte, or squeezes
the world in the press of its irony like the divine

Rabelais; or again, whether it jests at beings, instead
of insulting things, like Le Maréchal de Richelieu; or
better still perhaps, mocks both men and things at
once, like the most celebrated of our ambassadors. But
the profound genius of Don Juan Belvidero summed
up in advance all these geniuses. He made a jest of
everything. His life was one mockery which embraced men, things, institutions, and ideas. As to eternity, after having talked familiarly for half an hour
with the Pope Julius II., at the end of the conversation he said to him, laughing: "If it is absolutely necessary to choose, I would rather believe in God than
the Devil; power united to goodness always offers
more resources than the genius of evil."

"Yes, but it is God's will that we should do penance in this world . . ."

"Ah, you are always thinking of your indulgences,"
answered Belvidero. "Well, I have a whole existence
in reserve wherein to repent of the faults of my former life!"

"Ah! if you understand old age in that sense," said
the Pope, "you run a chance of canonization."

"After your elevation to the papacy all things are
credible." And they went to watch the workmen building the immense basilica dedicated to Saint Peter.

"Saint Peter is the man of genius who built up our
double power," said the Pope to Don Juan; "he de-
serves this monument. But sometimes at night I think
that a deluge will pass its sponge over it all, and the
world will have to begin again——"

Don Juan and the Pope began to laugh; they understood each other. A fool would have gone the next
day to enjoy himself with Julius II. at Raphael's or in

the delicious Villa-Madama; but Belvidero went to see him pontificate, in order to be convinced of his doubts. At an orgy, Della Rovere would have been capable of criticizing or confuting the Apocalypse.

However, I did not undertake this legend to furnish materials to those desirous of writing memoirs of the life of Don Juan; it is designed to prove to all decent people that Belvidero did not die in a duel with a stone, as some lithographers would have us believe. When Don Juan had reached the age of sixty he went and took up his abode in Spain. There in his old age, he married a young and lovely Andalusian, but he purposely made neither a good husband nor a good father. He had observed that we are never so tenderly loved as by women for whom we scarcely care at all. Doña Elvira had been piously brought up by an old aunt, in a castle some few leagues from San Lucar, in the wilds of Andalusia; she was a paragon of devotion and grace. Don Juan divined that this young girl would make a wife who would fight against passion for a long time before she yielded, so he hoped to be able to preserve her virtuous until his death. It was a grim jest, a game of chess which he had determined to reserve to play during his old age. Forewarned by all the mistakes of his father Bartolomeo, Don Juan resolved to make the least actions of his old age contribute to the success of the drama which was to be played out upon his death-bed. With this end in view, he buried the greater part of his riches in the cellars of his palace at Ferrara, which he seldom visited. As to the other half, he devoted it entirely to purchasing an annuity, in order that his wife and children might have an interest in the continuance of his life, a kind

of roguery which it would have been well for Don
Bartolomeo himself if he practiced; but for Don
Juan this Machiavellesque speculation was scarcely necessary. The young Felipe Belvidero grew up as con-
scientious and religious a Spaniard as his father was
impious, in virtue perhaps of the proverb: "A miser
breeds a spendthrift son."

The Abbot of San Lucar was chosen by Don Juan
to direct the consciences of the Duchess of Belvidero
and of Felipe. This ecclesiastic was a holy man, of
fine figure, admirably proportioned, with beautiful
black eyes; in fact, he had the head of a Tiberius,
fatigued with fasts, pale with penance, and tempted
daily as are all men who live in solitude. The old
noble hoped perhaps still to be able to kill a monk before finishing his first lease of life. But whether it
was that the priest was as strong as Don Juan himself, or that Doña Elvira possessed more prudence or
virtue than Spain usually bestows upon her daughters,
Don Juan was constrained to spend his last days like
an old country *curé* without a single scandal in his
house. At times he took pleasure in finding his son or
his wife at fault in their religious duties, for he willed
despotically that they should perform all the obligations imposed on the faithful by the Court of Rome.
In fact he was never so happy as when he was listening to the gallant priest, Doña Elvira, and Felipe engaged in discussing some point of conscience. However, in spite of the prodigious care which the Señor
Don Juan Belvidero bestowed upon his person, the
days of his decrepitude drew on; with this age of
trouble came the cries of impotence, cries the more
heartrending because of all the rich memories of his

turbulent youth and voluptuous manhood. This man, who had reached the last degree of cynicism—to induce others to believe in laws and principles at which he scoffed,—slept at night on the doubt of a perhaps!

This model of fine breeding, this aristocratic athlete in debauchery, this paragon of gallantry, this gracious flatterer of women whose hearts he had twisted as a peasant twists an osier band, this man of genius, was plagued with catarrh, pestered by sciatica, a martyr to the agonies of gout.

He saw his teeth depart, as the fairest and most beautifully dressed ladies depart one by one at the end of a fesitval and leave the halls empty and deserted. Then his sinuous hands trembled, his graceful legs tottered; at last one evening apoplexy squeezed his neck with her icy, crooked fingers. After this fatal day he became harsh and morose. He found fault with the devotion of his wife and son, asserting sometimes that the touching and delicate care which they lavished upon him was only given because he had sunk all his fortune in an annuity. Then Elvira and Felipe would shed bitter tears and redouble their caresses upon the malicious old man, and then his voice would grow affectionate to them and he would say: "My dear, my dear wife, you forgive me both, do you not? I tease you a little. Alas! good God! why dost Thou use me to try these two heavenly creatures? I, who ought to be their joy, I am their scourge."

In this way he chained them to his bedside, making them forget whole months of impatience and cruelty by one hour, when he would display for them ever new treasures of favor and false tenderness. This paternal system brought him infinitely more success than the system formerly used in his case by his father had brought him. At last he reached such a pitch of disease that, in order to put him to bed, they had to manœuver him like a felucca entering a dangerous channel. Then the day of his death arrived. This brilliant and sceptical personage, whose intellect alone survived the most horrible of all destructions, found himself between two antipathies, a physician and a confessor; but even with them he was gay. Was there not for him a light shining behind the veil of the future? Upon this veil—of lead to others, but transparent for him—the joyous, ravishing delights of youth played like shadows.

It was a beautiful summer evening when Don Juan felt the approach of death. The Spanish sky was exquisitely clear, the orange trees scented the air, the stars shed their bright and freshening beams, nature seemed to give him sure pledges for his resurrection, a pious and obedient son watched him with looks of respect and affection. About eleven o'clock he desired to be alone with this ingenuous youth.

"Felipe," said he, in a voice so tender and affectionate that the young man trembled and shed tears of joy. Never before had this stern father thus pronounced the word "Felipe." "Listen to me, my son," continued the dying man. "I am a great sinner. So during the whole of my life I have thought of my death. Formerly I was a friend of the great Pope Julius II. That illustrious Pontiff, fearing lest the excessive excitation of my senses should cause me to commit some mortal sin between the moment of my receiving the holy oils and my latest breath, made me a present of a phial in which there is preserved some

of the holy water which gushed out of the rock in the
desert. I have kept the secret of this diversion of the
treasure of the church, but I am authorized to reveal
this mystery to my son, *in articulo mortis.* You will
find this phial in the drawer of the Gothic table which
has always stood at my bedside. The precious crystal
will serve for you too, my beloved Felipe. Swear to
me on your eternal salvation to execute my orders
exactly."

Felipe looked at his father. Don Juan understood
the expression of human feeling too well not to die in
peace on the credit of such a look, just as his father
had died in despair on the credit of his.

"Thou deservest another father," replied Don Juan.
"I must confess to thee, my child, that at the moment
the worthy Abbot of San Lucar was administering the
viaticum to me, I thought of the incompatibility of
two powers as extensive as God's and the devil's."

"Oh! my father!"

"And I said to myself that, when Satan makes his
peace, he will be bound, unless he is a wretched scoun-
drel, to stipulate for the pardon of his adherents. This
thought haunts me. I shall go to hell, my son, if thou
dost not fulfil my wishes."

"Oh! tell me, father, quickly!"

"As soon as I have closed my eyes," replied Don
Juan, "which will be in a few minutes, perhaps, take
my body, even while it is still warm, and stretch it out
on a table in the middle of this room. Then extinguish
this lamp, the light of the stars will be sufficient for
thee. Strip me of my clothes; and while thou recitest
Paters and *Aves,* and raisest up thy soul to God, take
care to moisten, with this holy water, my eyes, my

lips, my whole head first, then all the members of my
body in succession; but, my dear son, the power of
God is so great, thou must not be astonished at anything!"

Here Don Juan, who felt death approaching, added
in a terrible voice:

"Hold the phial tight!" then expired gently in the
arms of a son whose tears ran in copious streams over
his pale, ironical countenance. It was about midnight
when Don Felipe Belvidero placed the corpse of his
father upon the table. After having kissed the menac-
ing brow and the gray locks, he extinguished the
lamp. The soft glow cast by the moonlight lit up the
country with its strange reflection, and allowed the
pious Felipe to see but indistinctly his father's corpse—
a something white amid the shade. The young man
steeped a cloth in the liquid, and—absorbed in prayer
meanwhile—faithfully anointed the venerated head
amidst profound silence. He certainly heard an indescribable shivering, but he attributed it to the play of
the breeze in the tree tops. When he had moistened
the right arm, he felt himself closely embraced round
the neck by a young and vigorous arm, and yet it was
his father's arm! A piercing shriek burst from his
lips, he dropped the phial, it broke;—the liquid evap-
orated. The servants of the castle came running in
armed with torches. This cry had terrified and as-
tounded them; it was as if the trumpet at the last judg-
ment had shaken the universe. In a moment the room
was full of people. The trembling crowd found Don
Felipe in a swoon, held by his father's powerful arm,
which clasped him round the neck. Then, marvelous
to relate, the assistants saw the head of Don Juan, as

young and beautiful as Antinoüs; a head with black
hair, and brilliant eyes, and ruddy mouth straining
horribly, and yet unable to move the skeleton to which
it belonged. An old serving man cried out, "A
miracle!" The Spaniards all repeated, "A miracle!"
Too pious to admit the mysteries of magic, Doña Elvira sent for the Abbot of San Lucar. When the
Abbot had seen the miracle with his own eyes, being
an Abbot who asked for nothing more than a chance
of augmenting his revenues, he resolved to profit by
it, like a man of sense. He declared at once that the
Señor Don Juan would undoubtedly be canonized, and
appointed the ceremony of his apotheosis at his monastery, which, he said, would be called henceforth San
Juan de Lucar. At these words the head made a very
funny grimace.

The taste of the Spaniards for this kind of solemnity
is so well known, that it ought not to be difficult to
imagine the religious fripperies with which the Abbey
of San Lucar celebrated the translation of the Blessed
Don Juan Belvidero into its Church. Within a few
days of the death of this illustrious Señor, the miracle
of his incomplete resurrection had been passed on so
briskly from village to village within a radius of more
than fifty leagues round San Lucar, that already it
was as good as a play to see the sightseers on the road;
they came from all sides scenting the delicacy of a *Te
Deum* chanted with flambeaux. The ancient mosque
of the monastery of San Lucar—a marvelous edifice
built by the Moors, whose vaults had heard for three
centuries the name of Jesus Christ substituted for the
name of Allah—could not contain the crowd come
together to witness the ceremony. Packed as close as

ants, Hidalgos, in velvet mantles, armed with their
good swords, stood upright round the pillars, finding
no room to bend knees that bent in no other place but
there; bewitching peasant girls, clad in basquines
which displayed their charms to advantage, gave their
arms to old white-haired men; young men, with passion in their eyes, found themselves side by side with
elderly decked-out women. Then there were couples
tremulous with happiness, curious maidens brought
thither by their sweethearts, brides and bridegrooms
married but a single night, children shyly holding one
another's hands. Such was the company, rich in color,
brilliant in contrast, laden with flowers and enamel,
making a soft hum of expectation in the silence of the
night. The wide doors of the Church opened. Those
who had come too late remained outside, and saw
from afar through the three open portals a scene of
which the vaporous decorations of our modern operas
could not give the faintest idea. Pious women and un-
holy men, eager to gain the good graces of a new saint,
lit thousands of tapers in his honor throughout the
vast Church—interested lights which made the building seem as if enchanted. The black arches, the
columns with their capitals, the deep chapels glittering
with gold and silver, the galleries, the Saracen carving,
the most delicate particles of this delicate scultpure
were outlined in this excess of light, like the capricious
figures formed in a glowing furnace. It was an ocean
of fire, dominated, at the end of the Church, by the
gilded choir, where towered the high altar rivalling in
its glory the rising sun. But the splendor of the
golden lamps, the silver candelabra, the tassels, the
saint and the *ex votos,* paled before the shrine wherein

lay Don Juan. The corpse of that impious person glistened with jewelry, and flowers, and crystals, and diamonds, and gold, and feathers as white as the wings of a seraph;—it replaced upon the altar a picture of Christ. About him glittered numberless tapers, which shot into the air their waves of lambent flame.

The worthy Abbot of San Lucar, vested in full pontificals, wearing his jewelled miter, his rochet, and golden cross, was enthroned on a seat of imperial splendor above the choir. All his clergy, aged and passionless men with silver hair, clad in albs of fine linen, were gathered round him, like the holy confessors whom painters group about the Eternal. The precentor and the dignitaries of the Chapter, decorated with their brilliant insignia and all their ecclesiastical vanities, passed to and fro in the shadowy depth of the incense, like the stars which roll through the firmament. When the hour of triumph was come, the bells awoke the echoes of the country, and this vast assembly raised to God the first cry of praise with which the *Te Deum* commences. It was indeed a sublime cry—voices clear and joyous, the voices of women in ecstasy, mingled with the deep, strong voices of men, those thousands of voices in so stupendous a chorus that the organ could not surpass it with all the roaring of its pipes. But amid this tumult of sound, the penetrating notes of the choristers and the sonorous tones of the basses evoked a train of gracious thought, representing childhood and strength in an impassioned concert of human voices blended in one sentiment of Love.

Te Deum laudamus!

From the midst of the Cathedral, black with the

kneeling multitude, this chant rose like a light that bursts forth suddenly in the night, and the silence was broken as by a roar of a thunder-clap. The voices ascended with the clouds of incense as they spread their blue, transparent veils upon the fantastic marvels of the architecture. All was splendor, perfume, light, and melody. At the moment when this anthem of love and thanksgiving rolled upward toward the altar, Don Juan, too polite not to return thanks, and too humorous not to understand a joke, answered by a terrible laugh, and drew himself up in his shrine. But the devil having put it into his head that he ran a chance of being taken for an ordinary individual, a saint, a *Boniface,* a *Pantaloon,* he threw this melody of love into confusion by a howling to which were added the thousand voices of Hell. Earth spoke her blessings, and Heaven uttered its curse. The ancient Church trembled to its foundations.

"*Te Deum laudamus!*" cried the assembly.

"Go to all the devils, brute beasts that you are! God, God! *Carajos Demonios,* idiotic creatures, with your silly old god!"

And a torrent of curses rolled out like a stream of burning lava in an eruption of Vesuvius.

"*Deus Sabaoth—Sabaoth!*" cried the Christians.

"You insult the majesty of Hell!" answered Don Juan, grinding his teeth.

Presently the living arm succeeded in getting free out of the shrine, and menaced the assembly with gestures eloquent of mockery and despair.

"The saint blesses us," said the old women, the children, and the maidens betrothed—a credulous people. Truly, we are often deceived in our worship. The man of power mocks at those who compliment him, and sometimes compliments those whom in the depth of his heart he mocks.

At that moment when the Abbot, prostrate before the altar, began to sing, *"Sancte Johannes, ora pro nobis!"* he heard quite distinctly, *"O coglione."*

"What's going on up there?" said the sub-prior, seeing the shrine move.

"The saint is playing the devil," answered the Abbot.

Then the living head detached itself violently from the body which lived no longer, and fell on the yellow skull of the officiant.

"Dost thou remember Doña Elvira?" it cried, fastening its teeth in the Abbot's head.

The Abbot uttered a terrible shriek, which threw the ceremony into confusion. All the priests ran up together and crowded round their superior.

"Idiot, say at least that there is a God!" screamed the voice. Just at that moment the Abbot, bitten in the brain, was about to expire.

CHRIST IN FLANDERS

CHRIST IN FLANDERS

AT a time somewhat indeterminate in Brabantine history, connection between the island of Cadzant and the coast of Flanders was kept up by a boat used for passengers to and fro. The capital of the island, Middleburg, afterward so celebrated in the annals of Protestantism, counted then hardly two or three hundred hearths. Rich Ostend was then an unknown harbor, flanked by a village thinly peopled by a few fisherfolk, and poor dealers, and pirates who plied their trade with impunity. Nevertheless, the borough of Ostend, composed of about twenty houses and three hundred cottages, cabins, and hovels—made with the remains of wrecked ships—rejoiced in a governor, a militia, a gallows, a convent, and a burgomaster, in fact, all the institutions of advanced civilization. Who was reigning at that time in Brabant, Belgium, and Flanders? 'On this point tradition is mute.

Let us admit that this story is strangely imbued with that vagueness, indefiniteness, and love of the marvelous, which the favorite orators of Flemish vigils love to intermingle in their legends, as varied in poetry as they are contradictory in detail. Told from age to age, repeated from hearth to hearth, by grandmothers and by story-tellers night and day, this chronicle has received each century a different color-

53

ing. Like those buildings planned according to the architectural caprice of each epoch, whose dark, crumbling masses are a pleasure to poets alone, this legend would drive commentators, and wranglers over facts, words, and dates, to desperation. The narrator believes in it, as all superstitious souls in Flanders have believed in it, without being for that reason either more learned or more weak-minded. Only in the impossibility of harmonizing all the different versions, here is the story, stripped perhaps of its romantic *naïveté*—for this it is impossible to reproduce—but still, with its daring statements disproved by history, and its morality approved by religion, its fantastic flowers of imagination, and hidden sense which the wise can interpret each to his own liking. Let each one seek his pasture therein and take the trouble to separate the good grain from the tares.

The boat which served to carry over the passengers from the island of Cadzant to Ostend was just about to leave the village. Before undoing the iron chain which held his boat to a stone on the little jetty where people embarked, the skipper blew his horn several times to call the loiterers, for this journey was his last. Night was coming on, the last fires of the setting sun scarcely gave enough light to distinguish the coast of Flanders or the tardy passengers on the island wandering along the earthen walls which surrounded the fields or among the tall reeds of the marshes. The boat was full. "What are you waiting for? Let us be off!" they cried. Just then a man appeared a few steps from the jetty. The pilot, who had neither heard nor seen him approaching, was somewhat surprised. The passenger seemed to have risen

from the earth on a sudden. He might have been a
peasant sleeping in a field, waiting for the hour for
starting, whom the horn had wakened up. Was it a
thief, or was it some one from the Custom House or
police? When he arrived on the jetty to which the
boat was moored, seven persons who were standing in
the stern hastened to sit down on the benches, in
order to have them to themselves and prevent the
stranger from seating himself among them. It was a
sudden instinctive feeling, one of those aristocratic in-
stincts which suggest themselves to rich people. Four
of these personages belonged to the highest nobility of
Flanders.

First of all, there was a young cavalier, with two
beautiful grayhounds, wearing over his long hair a
cap decked with jewels. He clinked his gilded spurs,
and now and again curled his mustache, as he cast disdainful looks at the rest of the freight.

Then there was a proud damosel, who carried a fal-
con on her wrist and spoke only to her mother or an
ecclesiastic of high rank, a relative, no doubt. These.
persons made as much noise talking together as if they
were the only people on the boat. All the same, next
to them sat a man of great importance in the country,
a fat merchant from Bruges, enveloped in a large
mantle. His servant, armed to the teeth, kept by his
side two bags full of money. Beside them was a man
of science, a doctor of the University of Louvain, with
his clerk. These people, who all despised one another,
were separated from the bows by the rower's bench.

When the late passenger put his foot into the boat
he gave a swift look at the stern, but when he saw no
room there he went to seek a place among the people in

the bows. It was the poor who sat there. At the sight
of a man bareheaded, whose brown cloth coat and fine
linen shirt had no ornament, who held in his hand
neither hat nor cap, with neither purse nor rapier at his
girdle, all took him for a burgomaster—a good and
gentle man, like one of those old Flemings whose
nature and simple character have been so well rendered
by the painters of their country. The poor passengers
welcomed the stranger with a respectful demeanor,
which excited mocking whispers among the people in
the stern. An old soldier, a man of toil and trouble,
gave him his place on the bench, and sat himself at the
end of the boat, keeping himself steady by putting his
feet against one of the transverse beams which knit the
planks together like the backbone of a fish.

A young woman, a mother with her little child, who
seemed to belong to the working-class of Ostend,
moved back to make room for the newcomer. In this
movement there was no trace either of servility or disdain. It was merely a mark of that kindliness by
which the poor, who know so well how to appreciate
a service, show their frank and natural disposition—so
simple and obvious in the expression of all their qualities, good or bad.

The stranger thanked them with a gesture full of
nobility, and sat down between the young mother and
the old soldier. Behind him was a peasant with his
son, ten years old. A poor old woman, with a wallet
almost empty, old and wrinkled, and in rags—a type
of misery and neglect—lay in the prow, crouched upon
a coil of ropes. One of the rowers, an old sailor, who
had known her when she was rich and beautiful, had
let her get in for what the people so beautifully call

"the love of God." "Thank you kindly, Thomas;"
the old woman had said; "I will say two *Paters* and
two *Aves* for you in my prayers this evening."

The skipper blew his horn once more, looked at the
silent country, cast the chain into his boat, ran along
the side to the helm, took the tiller, and stood erect;
then, having looked at the sky, called out in a loud
voice to the rowers, when they were well in the open
sea, "Row hard, make haste; the sea smiles evilly—
the witch! I feel the swell at the helm and the storm
at my wound." These words, spoken in the language
of the sea—a tongue only understood of those accustomed to the sound of the waves—gave to the oars a
hastened but ever-cadenced movement, as different
from the former manner of rowing as the gallop of a
horse from its trot. The fine people sitting at the
stern took pleasure in seeing the sinuous arms, the
bronzed faces with eyes of fire, the distended muscles,
and the different human forms working in unison, just
to get them the quicker over this narrow strait. So
far from being sorry for their labor, they pointed out
the rowers to each other, and laughed at the grotesque
expressions which their exertion printed on their anxious faces. In the prow the soldier, the peasant, and the
old woman, regarded the mariners with that kind of
compassion natural to people who, living by toil, know
its hard anguish and feverish fatigue. Besides, being
accustomed to life in the open air, they all divined by
the look of the sky the danger which threatened them;
so they were serious. The young mother was rocking
her child to sleep, singing to it some old hymn of the
church.

"If we do get over," said the old soldier to the peasant, "God will have taken a great deal of trouble to keep us alive."

"Ah! He is master," said the old woman; "but I think it is His good pleasure to call us to Himself. Do you see that light, there?" and by a gesture of the head she pointed out the setting sun. Bands of fire streaked vividly the brown-red tinted clouds, which seemed just about to unchain a furious wind. The sea gave forth a suppressed murmur, a sort of internal groan, something like the growling of a dog whose anger will not be appeased.

After all Ostend was not far off. Just now the sky and the sea showed one of those sights to which it is impossible for words or painting to give longer duration than they have in reality. Human creations like powerful contrasts, so artists generally demand from nature its most brilliant aspects, despairing perhaps to be able to render the great and beautiful poetry of her . ordinary appearance, although the human soul is often as profoundly moved by calm as by motion, by the silence as much as by the storm.

There was one moment when every one on the boat was silent and gazed on the sea and sky, whether from presentiment or in obedience to that religious melancholy which comes over nearly all of us at the hour of prayer, at the fall of day, at the moment when nature is silent and the bells speak. The sea cast up a faint, white glimmer, but changing like the color of steel; the sky was mostly gray; in the west long, narrow spaces looked like waves of blood, whereas in the east glittering lines, marked as by a fine pencil, were separated from one another by clouds, folded like the wrinkles on an old man's forehead. Thus the sea and the sky formed a neutral background, everything in half tints, which made the fires of the setting sun glare ominously. The face of nature inspired a feeling of terror. If it is allowable to interweave the daring hyperboles of the people into the written language, one might repeat what the soldier said, "Time is rolling away," or what the peasant answered, that the sky had the look of a hangman. All of a sudden the wind rose in the west, and the skipper, who never ceased to watch the sea, seeing it swell toward the horizon, cried, "Ho, ho!" At this cry the sailors stopped immediately, and let their oars float.

"The skipper's right," said Thomas. The boat, borne on the top of a huge wave, seemed to be descending to the bottom of the gaping sea. At this extraordinary movement and this sudden rage of the ocean the people in the stern turned pale, and gave a terrible cry, "We perish!"

"Not yet," answered the skipper quietly. At this moment the clouds were rent in twain by the force of the wind exactly above the boat. The gray masses spread out with ominous quickness from east to west, and the twilight, falling straight down through a rent made by the storm-wind, rendered visible every face. The passengers, the rich and the noble, the sailors and the poor, all stopped one moment in astonishment at the aspect of the last comer. His golden hair, parted in the middle on his tranquil, serene forehead, fell in many curls on his shoulders, and outlined against the gray sky a face sublime in its gentleness, radiant with divine love. He did not despise death; he was certain not to perish. But if at first the people at the stern had forgotten for an instant the tempest whose implacable fury menaced them, they soon returned to their selfish sentiments and lifelong habits.

"It's lucky for him, that dolt of a burgomaster, that he does not know the danger we are all in. There he stands like a dog, and doesn't seem to mind dying," said the doctor.

Hardly had he completed this judicious remark when the tempest unchained its lesions; wind blew from every side, the boat spun round like a top, and the sea swamped it.

"Oh, my poor child! my child! who will save my child?" cried the mother, in a heartrending voice.

"You yourself," replied the stranger. The sound of this voice penetrated the heart of the young woman and put hope therein. She heard this sweet word, in spite of the raging of the storm, in spite of the shrieks of the passengers.

"Holy Virgin of Perpetual Succor, who art at Antwerp, I promise you twenty pounds of wax and a statue if you will only get me out of this," cried the merchant, falling on his knees upon his bags of gold.

"The Virgin is no more at Antwerp than she is here," replied the doctor.

"She is in heaven," said a voice, which seemed to come forth from the sea.

"Who spoke?"

"The devil," said the servant; "he's mocking the Virgin of Antwerp."

"Shut up with your blessed Virgin," said the skipper to the passengers; "take hold of the bowls and help me get the water out of the boat. As to you," he continued, addressing the sailors, "row hard, we have a moment's grace, and in the devil's name, who has

left you in this world until now, let us be our own
Providence. This little strip of water is horribly dangerous, I know from thirty years' experience. Is this
evening the first time I have had a storm to deal with?"
Then standing at the helm, the skipper continued to
look alternately at the boat, the sea, and the sky.

"The skipper mocks at everything," said Thomas in
a low voice.

"Will God let us die with these wretched people?"
asked the proud damosel of the handsome cavalier.

"No! no! Noble damosel, listen to me." He put his
arm round her waist, and spoke in her ear. "I can
swim—don't say anything about it; I will take you by
your beautiful hair and bring you safely to the shore;
but I can save you only."

The damosel looked at her old mother; the dame was
on her knees asking absolution from the bishop, who
was not listening to her. The cavalier read in the eyes
of his beautiful mistress some faint sentiment of filial
piety, so he said to her in a low voice, "Submit yourself to the will of God; if He wishes to call your
mother to Himself, it will be doubtless for her happiness—in the other world," he added, in a voice still
lower, "and for ours in this."

The dame Rupelmonde possessed seven fiefs, besides
the barony of Gavres. The damosel listened to the
voice of life, to the interests of love, speaking by the
mouth of the handsome adventurer, a young mis-
creant, who haunted churches, seeking for prey—either
a girl to marry or else good ready money.

The light, which lit up the pale faces, showed all
their varying expressions, when the boat was borne up
into the air by a wave, or cast down to the bottom of the

abyss; then, shaken like a frail leaf, a plaything of the autumn wind, it cracked its shell, and seemed nigh to break altogether. Then there were horrible cries alternating with awful silence.

The demeanor of the people seated in the prow of the boat contrasted singularly with that of the rich and powerful in the stern. The young mother strained her child to her bosom every time that the waves threatened to engulf the frail bark; but she held to the hope with which the words of the stranger had filled her heart: each time she turned her eyes toward this man she drank in from his face a new faith, the strong faith of a weak woman, the faith of a mother. Living by the divine word, the word of love, which had gone forth from this man, the simple creature awaited trustfully the fulfilment of the sort of promise he had given her, and scarcely feared the tempest any more. Sticking to the side of the boat, the soldier ceased not to contemplate this singular being, on whose impassibility he sought to model his own rough, tanned face, bringing into play all his intelligence and strength of will, whose powerful springs had not been vitiated in the course of a passive mechanical life. He was emulous to show himself tranquil and calm. After the manner of this superior courage, he ended by identifying himself in some measure with the secret principle of its interior power. Then his imagination became an instinctive fanaticism, a love without limit, a faith in this man, like that enthusiasm which soldiers have for their commander when he is a man of power, surrounded with the glory of victories, marching in the midst of the splendid prestige of genius. The poor old woman said in a low voice, "Ah! what a miserable sinner I am! Have I not suffered enough to expiate the pleasures of my youth? Miserable one, why hast thou led the gay life of a Frenchwoman? Why hast thou consumed the goods of God with the people of the Church, the goods of the poor 'twixt the drink shop and the pawn shop? Ah! how wicked I was! Oh! my God! my God! let me finish my hell in this world of misery. Holy Virgin, Mother of God, take pity on me."

"Console yourself, mother, God is not a Lombard; although I have killed here and there good people and wicked, I do not fear for the resurrection."

"Ah! Sir, how happy they are, those beautiful ladies who are near the bishop, holy man!" the old woman went on; "they will have absolution from their sins. Oh! if I could only hear the voice of a priest saying to me, 'Your sins are forgiven you,' I could believe him."

The stranger turned toward her, and his look, full of charity, made her tremble. "Have faith," he said, "and you will be saved."

"May God reward you, good sir," she answered. "If you speak truly, I will go for you and for me on a pilgrimage to Our Lady of Loretto, barefooted."

The two peasants, father and son, remained silent, resigned, and submitting to the will of God, as people accustomed to follow instinctively, like animals, the convulsions of nature.

So on one side there were riches, pride, knowledge, debauchery, crime, all human society such as it is made by arts, thought, and education, the world and its laws; but also on this side, only shrieks, terror, the struggles of a thousand conflicting feelings, with horrible doubt—naught but the anguish of fear. And, towering above these, one powerful man, the skipper of the boat, doubting nothing, the chief, the fatalist king, making his own Providence, crying out for bailing-bowls and not on the Virgin to save him, defying the storm, and wrestling with the sea, body to body.

At the other end of the boat, the weak :—the mother, holding to her bosom a little child, who smiled at the storm :—a wanton once gay, now given over to horrible remorse :—a soldier, scarred with wounds, without other reward than his mutilated life, as a price for indefatigable devotion; he had hardly a morsel of bread, steeped in tears; all the same, he laughed at everything, and marched on without care, happy when he could drown his glory at the bottom of a pot of beer, or was telling stories thereof to wondering children. He commended gaily to God the care of his future. Lastly, two peasants, people of toil and weariness, labor incarnate, the work on which the world lives; these simple creatures were guileless of thought and its treasures, but ready to lose themselves utterly in a belief; having a more robust faith, in that they had never discussed or analyzed it; virgin natures, in whom conscience had remained pure and feeling strong. Contrition, misery, love, work had exercised, purified, concentrated, disculpated their will, the only thing which in man resembles that which sages call the soul.

When the boat, piloted by the marvelous dexterity of the skipper, came almost in view of Ostend, fifty paces from the shore, it was driven back by the convulsion of the storm, and suddenly began to sink. The stranger with the light upon his face then said to this little world of sorrow, "Those who have faith shall be saved; let them follow me." This man stood up and walked with a firm step on the waves. At once the young mother took her child in her arms and walked with him on the sea. The soldier suddenly stood at attention, saying in his rough language, "By my pipe! I will follow you to the devil." Then, without seeming astonished, he marched on the sea.

The old prostitute, believing in the omnipotence of God, followed the man, and walked on the sea. The two peasants said, "As they are walking on the sea, why should not we?" So they got up and hastened after the others, walking on the sea.

Thomas wished to do likewise; but his faith wavered, and he fell several times into the sea, but got out again; and after three failures he too walked upon the sea.

The daring pilot stuck like a leech to the bottom of his boat. The merchant had faith, and had risen, but he wanted to take his gold with him, and his gold took him to the bottom of the sea. Mocking at the charlatan and the imbeciles who listened to him, at the moment when he saw the stranger proposing to the passengers to walk on the sea, the man of science began to laugh, and was swallowed up in the ocean. The damosel was drawn down into the abyss by her lover. The bishop and the old lady went to the bottom, heavy with sin perhaps, heavier still with unbelief and confidence in false images; heavy with devotional practices, light of alms and true religion.

The faithful troop, who trod with firm, dry feet on the plain of the raging waters, heard around them the horrible howling of the storm; great sheets of water broke in their path; irresistible force rent the ocean in twain. Through the mist these faithful ones per--

ceived on the shore a little feeble light, which flickered in the window- of a fisherman's cabin. Each one as he marched bravely toward this light seemed to hear his neighbor crying through the roaring sea, "Courage!" Nevertheless, absorbed each in his own danger, no one said a single word. And so they reached the shore. When they were all seated at the hearth of the fisherman, they sought in vain the guide who had a light upon his face. Seated upon the summit of a rock, at the base of which the hurricane had cast the pilot, stuck to his plank with all the strength of a sailor in the throes of death, the MAN descended, picked up the shipwrecked man almost dashed to pieces; then he said, as he held out a helping hand over his head, "It is well this once, but do as thou hast done no more; the example would be too bad." He took the mariner on his shoulders, and carried him to the fisherman's cottage. He knocked for the unfortunate man, that one should open to him the door of this humble refuge; then the Savior disappeared.

In this place the sailors built the Convent of Mercy, where were long to be seen the prints that the feet of JESUS CHRIST had, it was said, left on the sand.

Afterward, when the French entered Belgium, some monks took away with them this precious relic, the testimony of the last visit JESUS ever paid to the earth.

IN THE TIME OF THE TERROR

IN THE TIME OF THE TERROR

On January 22, 1793, about eight o'clock in the evening, an old lady was walking down the steep incline which ends in front of the Church of Saint Laurent in Paris. It had snowed so hard all day that her footsteps were scarcely audible. The streets were deserted, and the feeling of fear which silence naturally inspires was increased by the remembrance of the terror under which France then groaned. The old lady had met no one on the way, and her eyesight, which had long been failing, did not allow of her distinguishing in the lamplight the few passers-by, scattered here and there like shadows along the immense vista of the *faubourg*. She went on bravely alone through the solitude, as if her age were a talisman to preserve her from all harm. When she had passed the Rue des Morts, she thought she could distinguish the firm, heavy tread of a man walking behind her. She fancied it was not the first time that she had heard the sound. She was afraid, thinking that she was being followed, so she tried to walk faster than before, in order to reach a shop-window in which the lights were bright enough for her to test the truth of her suspicions. As soon as she found herself in the gleam of light which streamed out horizontally from the shop she turned her head suddenly and perceived a

69

human form in the mist. This indistinct glimpse was
enough; a feeling of terror fell upon her; she tottered
for a moment under it, for now she felt certain that
this stranger had accompanied her from the first step
she had taken outside her own house. Her desire to
escape from this spy gave her strength; incapable of
reasoning, she walked twice as fast as before, as
though it were possible for her to distance a man necessarily much more active than she. After running
for some minutes, she reached a pastry-cook's shop,
went in and fell, rather than sat down, on a chair
which was standing before the counter. As her hand
rattled upon the latch a young woman seated at her
embroidery raised her eyes from her work, looked
through the square pane of glass, and recognized the
old-fashioned violet silk mantle which enveloped the
old lady; then she hurriedly opened a drawer, as if
to take out something that she had been keeping there
for her. Not only did this movement and the expression of the young woman's face betray her desire to
get rid of the stranger as soon as possible, as a person
whom she did not want to see, but she even let a gesture
of impatience escape her when she found the drawer
empty. Then, without looking at the lady, she went
out hastily from behind the counter into the back part
of the shop and called her husband; he appeared at
once.

"Wherever have you put—?" she asked, mysteriously, glancing in the direction of the old lady, and not
finishing the sentence.

The pastry-cook could only see the old lady's head-
dress, a huge black bonnet, trimmed with violet ribands, but he looked at his wife as much as to say, "Do

you think I should leave a thing like that in your counter?" and disappeared. His wife, surprised that the old lady sat so still and silent, went close up to her; when she saw her she was seized with a feeling of compassion, and perhaps of curiosity too. Although the old lady's face was naturally pallid, like the face of a person who practices austerities in secret, it was easy to see that some recent emotion had rendered it even more pallid than usual. Her head-dress was so arranged as to hide her hair, which was white, no doubt from age, for it was evident that she did not wear powder, as there was no sign of it upon the collar of her dress. This absence of ornament gave her face a look of religious severity. Her features were proud and grave. In former times the manners and habits of people of rank were so different from those of the other classes that it was easy then to distinguish a noble. Thus the young woman felt sure that the strange lady was a *ci-devant,* who had at one time been attached to the Court.

"Madame?" said she involuntarily, forgetting, in the respect she inspired, that the title was proscribed.

The old lady made no answer; she kept her eyes fixed on the shop-window, as if some terrible object were depicted on the glass.

"What is the matter, *citoyenne?*" asked the shopman, returning at that moment.

The worthy pastry-cook awoke the lady from her reverie, by handing her a small cardboard box wrapt up in blue paper.

"Nothing, nothing, my friends," said she in a gentle voice.

She raised her eyes to the pastry-cook, as if to thank

him by a look; but seeing a red cap upon his head, she
cried aloud—

"Ah! you have betrayed me!"

The young woman and her husband answered with
a gesture of horror; the stranger blushed, either with
relief, or with regret at having suspected them.

"Forgive me!" she said at once, with childish sweetness. Then she drew a gold *louis* out of her pocket
and gave it to the pastry-cook. "That is the price we
agreed upon," said she. There is a state of want recognized instinctively by those in want themselves. The
pastry-cook and his wife looked at one another, inter-
changing the same thought as they glanced at the old
lady. The *louis* was evidently her last. Her hands
trembled as she held out the coin to them; he looked at it
sorrowfully, but without grudging, though she seemed
to be conscious of the full extent of the sacrifice. Hunger and misery were engraved upon her face in as
legible characters as her ascetic habits and her present fear. Her clothes still bore the traces of past richness. She was dressed in faded silk, with carefully
mended lace, and an elegant though worn mantle—in
fact, the rags of former wealth. The shop-keepers,
wavering between pity and self-interest, tried to soothe
their conscience with words.

"*Citoyenne,* you seem very poorly."

"Would Madame like to take anything?" asked the
woman, catching up her husband's words.

"We've got some very good broth," said the pastry-
cook.

"It's so cold, perhaps you have caught a chill,
Madame, coming here; you are welcome to rest a bit
and warm yourself."

"We are not so black as the devil," said the pastry-cook.

Reassured by the friendly tone of the charitable pastry-cook, the lady admitted that she had been followed by a man, and was afraid to go home alone.

"Is that all?" replied the man with the red cap. "Wait a minute for me, *citoyenne*."

He gave the *louis* to his wife; then, moved by that sense of acknowledgment which steals into the heart of a vendor who has received an exorbitant price for goods of slight value, he went and put on his uniform as a *guarde national*, took his hat and sword, and returned under arms. But his wife had had time to reflect. As in many other hearts, reflection closed the hand which benevolence had opened. The woman had got frightened; she was afraid her husband would get into some scrape, so she plucked at the lappet of his coat to detain him. However, in obedience to an instinct of charity, the good man offered on the spot to escort the old lady.

"It looks as if the man whom the *citoyenne* is afraid of were still prowling round the shop," said the young woman sharply.

"I am afraid he is," frankly admitted the lady.

"Suppose it were a spy? or perhaps there is a conspiracy! Do not go—and take the box away from her."

These words were whispered into the pastry-cook's ear by his wife; they froze the extempore courage which had inflated his breast.

"Eh! I'll just go and say a word to him, and he'll be off in a minute," he exclaimed, opening the door and going out precipitately.

The old lady sat down again on her chair as passive
as a child; she looked almost silly. The honest shopman speedily returned; his face, red enough to begin
with, and further inflamed by the fire of his oven, had
suddenly become livid; he was so overcome with terror that his legs tottered under him, and his eyes looked
like a drunkard's.

"D'you want to get our heads cut off, wretched
aristocrat!" he cried, furious. "Come, take to your
heels, and don't ever show yourself here again. Don't
expect me to furnish you with the elements of conspiracy!"

As the pastry-cook finished these words, he tried to
snatch back the little box, which the old lady had put
into one of her pockets. But scarcely had the im-
pudent fellow's hands touched her clothes, when the
strange lady—preferring to face the dangers of her
walk unprotected save by God, rather than lose that
she had just purchased—regained all the agility of her
youth; she sprang to the door, opened it suddenly, and
vanished from the gaze of the pastry-cook and his
wife, leaving them trembling and stupefied. As soon
as she found herself outside, she set off at a quick
walk; but her strength soon failed her, for she heard
the heavy footsteps of the spy who was following her
so pitilessly, crunching the snow behind her. She was
obliged to stop; he stopped too. Whether from fear
or lack of intelligence, she did not dare either to speak
or to look at him. She went on, walking slowly; then
the man slackened his steps, always keeping at a distance from which he was able to watch her. The
stranger seemed to be the very shadow of the woman.
Nine o'clock struck as this silent pair passed again be-

fore the Church of Saint Laurent. It is in the nature
of every heart, even the feeblest, that a feeling of calmness should succeed to violent agitation, for, if feeling
is infinite, our organization is limited. So the strange
woman, as she experienced no harm from her sup-
posed persecutor, was inclined to look upon him as an
unknown friend anxious to protect her. She summed
up all the circumstances attendant on the apparitions
of the stranger with a view to discover plausible cor-
roboration of this consoling theory; she was bent on
finding out good intentions in him rather than evil.
Forgetting the terror with which he had inspired the
pastry-cook just before, she passed on with a firm step
through the higher parts of le faubourg Saint Martin. After walking for half an hour, she reached a
house situated at the corner formed by the principal
street of the *faubourg* and the street which leads to la
barrière de Pantin. Even now this is still one of the
loneliest places in the whole of Paris. The north wind
blows over les buttes de Saint Chaumont and de Belle-
ville, and whistles through the houses—or rather
hovels—sprinkled over a nearly deserted valley,
divided by walls of mud and bones. This desolate
spot seemed the natural refuge of misery and despair.
The man, implacable in his pursuit of this poor creature, who was yet bold enough to traverse those silent
streets by night, seemed impressed by the scene that
rose before him. He stopped to consider, standing upright in an attitude of hesitation. A lamp, whose
flickering flame could scarcely penetrate the mist, cast
its faint light upon him. Fright gave the old woman
eyes. She thought she could descry a sinister look
upon the man's features. She felt her fears reawaken-

ing,—then, taking advantage of a sort of uncertainty which seemed to make him linger, she glided through the darkness to the door of the solitary house, touched a spring, and was gone swift as a dream. The man stood motionless looking at the house. In a certain measure it might have served for the type of the wretched dwellings of this *faubourg*. The crazy cabin was built of ashlar smeared with a coat of plaster, so rotten and with such big cracks that it looked as if the least puff of wind would blow the whole thing down. The roof, covered with brown moss-grown tiles, had sunk in several places, and seemed on the point of falling in under the weight of the snow. There were three windows in each story, the frames mouldering with damp and starting with the action of the sun; it was evident that the cold must find its way through them into the rooms. The house was as isolated as an ancient tower that time has forgotten to destroy. The attics at the top of the wretched building were pierced with windows at irregular intervals, and from these shone a dim light, but the rest of the house was in complete darkness. The old woman had some difficulty in climbing the rough awkward staircase, up which a rope served for a handrail. She knocked mysteriously at the door of a lodging in the attic; an old man offered her a chair; she sat down in it precipitately.

"Hide! hide!" said she. "Though we only go out so seldom, they know everything we do, and spy out every step we take."

"What is it now?" asked another old woman who was sitting by the fire.

"The man who has been prowling round the house

since yesterday morning has been following me this evening."

At these words the three inhabitants of the garret looked at each other; they did not try to conceal the signs of profound terror visible on their faces. The old man was the least agitated of the three, perhaps because he was in the most danger. A brave man under the burden of great misfortune or under the yoke of persecution, has already—so to speak—begun his self-sacrifice; he looks upon each day of his life only as one more victory gained over fate. It was easy to see from the looks of the two women which were fastened on the old man that he and he alone was the object of their intense anxiety.

"Why should we cease to trust in God, sisters?" said he in a hollow voice, but with much earnestness; "we sang His praises amid the shouts of the murderers and the cries of the dying in the Carmelite Convent; if He willed that I should be saved from the massacre, it was doubtless to preserve me for a destiny that I must endure without murmuring. God protects His own, He can dispose of them according to His will. It is you we must take thought for, not for me."

"No," said one of the two old women, "what is our life compared with the life of a priest?"

"When I was once outside the Abbaye de Chelles I looked upon myself as dead," exclaimed the nun who had not been out. "Look," said the one who had just come in, "here are the Hosts." "But," she exclaimed, "I can hear some one coming up the stairs."

At these words they all three listened; the noise ceased.

"Do not be alarmed," said the priest, "if some one tries to find you. Some one, on whose fidelity we can count, was to take all necessary steps for crossing the frontier, and will come for letters which I have written to le Duc de Langeais and le Marquis de Beauséant, asking them to consider means for rescuing you from this terrible country, and the death or misery which awaits you here."

"But will you not follow us?" whispered the two nuns eagerly, with a sort of despair.

"My place is where there are victims," said the priest simply.

The women looked at their guest in silence, with holy admiration.

"Sœur Marthe," said he, addressing the sister who had gone out for the Hosts, "this messenger will answer *Fiat voluntas* to the word *Hosanna.*"

"There is some one on the stairs!" exclaimed the other nun, opening a hiding-place contrived under the roof.

This time, in the profound silence, they could easily hear the steps, which were covered with lumps of dried mud, creaking under the tread of a man. The priest squeezed with difficulty into a sort of wardrobe, and the nun threw some clothes over him.

"You can shut the door, Sœur Agathe," said he in a muffled voice.

He was scarcely hidden when there were three raps at the door. The two holy women trembled; they took counsel by looks, not daring to pronounce a single word. They appeared to be both about sixty years old. Cut off from the world for forty years, they were like plants accustomed to the atmosphere of a greenhouse,

which die if they are put out of it. They were so
habituated to convent life that they could not conceive
any other. One morning their gratings had been
broken down, and they had shuddered at finding themselves free. It is easy to picture the sort of unnatural
numbness that the events of the Revolution had produced in their innocent hearts. Incapable of recon-
ciling their monastic ideas with the difficulties of life,
they could not even understand their own situation;
they were like children who have been once cared for
and then abandoned by their special providence—their
mother, praying instead of crying. Thus in the face
of the danger they foresaw at this moment, they remained mute and passive, knowing no other defence
than Christian resignation. The man who had asked
for admittance interpreted their silence as consent; he
opened the door at once and presented himself. The
two nuns shuddered when they recognized him as the
person who had been prowling round their house for
some time past collecting information about them.
They sat motionless, looking at him with apprehensive
curiosity, like a shy child silently staring at a stranger.
The man was stout and of lofty stature; there was
nothing in his bearing, his manner, or his physiog-
nomy suggestive of an evil nature. He imitated the
stillness of the nuns, while his eyes slowly examined
the room he had just entered.

Two straw mats, placed on the bare boards, served
as beds for the two nuns; there was only one table, in
the middle of the room; on it stood some plates, three
knives, and a round loaf; a small fire burned in the
grate; some pieces of wood piled up in a corner bore
further witness to the poverty of the two recluses.

The walls were covered with a layer of very old paint, showing the bad condition of the roof by the stains upon it, which marked with brown streams the infiltration of the rain. A relic, no doubt rescued from the village of the Abbaye de Chelles, was placed like an ornament upon the mantelpiece. Three chairs, two chests, and a wretched cupboard completed the furniture of the room, but a door near the fireplace suggested that there might be a second.

The person who had introduced himself under such terrible auspices into the bosom of this family did not take long to make an inventory of their cell. His features assumed an expression of pity as he cast a look of benevolence upon the two women; he was at least as embarrassed as they. The strange silence which they all three kept did not last long, for presently the stranger began to comprehend the moral feebleness and inexperience of the two poor creatures, so he said to them in a voice which he tried to make gentle: "I am not come to you, as an enemy, *citoyennes*—" He stopped short, and then went on: *"Mes sœurs,* if any misfortune should happen to you, believe me it is not I who will have contributed to it. I have a favor to ask of you."

They still kept silence.

"If I intrude upon you—if I annoy you, tell me so freely—I will leave you; but I hope you will understand that I am entirely devoted to you; that if there is any service I could render you, you may command me without fear, for I alone, perhaps—now that there is no king—am above the law."

There was a ring of truth in his words. Sœur Agathe, the nun who belonged to the family of Langeais, and whose manners seemed to show that she had formerly been familiar with brilliant society and had breathed the air of a court, hastened to point to a chair, as if to invite their visitor to sit down. The stranger showed a sort of pleasure mingled with sadness when he saw this gesture; then he waited to sit down until the two worthy ladies had done so themselves.

"You have given refuge," he went on, "to a venerable priest who has not taken the oaths, who escaped miraculously from a massacre of the Carmelites."

"*Hosanna!*" said Sœur Agathe, interrupting him, and looking at him with nervous curiosity.

"No, I do not think that is his name," he replied.

"But Monsieur," said Sœur Marthe eagerly, "we have not got any priest here; and——"

"Then you should have been more prudent and wary," answered the stranger, stretching out his hand and taking a breviary from the table. "I do not think that you are likely to know Latin, and——"

He did not go on; the extraordinary emotion expressed by the faces of the poor nuns made him afraid he had gone too far; they trembled, and their eyes filled with tears.

"Do not distress yourselves," he said frankly. "I know the name of your guest and your own; three days ago I learned all about your distress, and your devotion to the venerable Abbé de——"

"Sh!" said Sœur Agathe simply, putting her finger to her lips.

"You see, *mes sœurs,* that if I had conceived the horrible plan of betraying you, I might have already accomplished it more than once."

When the priest heard these words he extricated himself from his prison, and appeared in the middle of the room.

"I cannot believe, Monsieur," said he to the strange man, "that you are one of our persecutors; I trust myself to you. What is it that you want of me?"

The holy confidence of the priest, the noble fervor expressed in all his features, would have disarmed a murderer. The mysterious person who had thus brought excitement into this scene of misery and resignation sat for a moment looking at the group of the three before him; then, assuming a confidential tone, he addressed the priest thus: *"Mon père,* I came to entreat you to celebrate a requiem mass for the repose of the soul of—of a—of a consecrated person whose body will never rest in hallowed ground." The priest shuddered involuntarily. The two nuns, not yet comprehending to whom the stranger referred, remained in an attitude of curiosity, their necks stretched out and their faces turned to the two speakers. The ecclesiastic scrutinized the man; genuine anxiety was visible in his face, and his eyes expressed ardent supplication.

"Eh bien! Come back to-night, at midnight; I shall be ready to celebrate the only funeral office we can offer in expiation of the crime of which you speak."

The stranger trembled, but he looked as if some feeling of satisfaction, at once solemn and sweet, had triumphed over some secret sorrow. After respectfully saluting the priest and the two holy women, he departed with an expression of mute gratitude understood by these three generous hearts. About two hours after this scene, he returned, knocked cautiously at the outer door of the attic, and was received by

Mademoiselle de Beauséant and led into the second room of their humble retreat. Here all had been prepared for the ceremony. Between the two pillars of the chimney-piece the nun had pushed up the old cupboard; its antique shape was hidden under a magnificent altar frontal of green *moire*. A large ebony and ivory crucifix was fastened to the yellow wall, making the bareness only more apparent, and of necessity attracting the eye to itself. The sisters had managed to set up four little slender tapers upon this temporary altar, by fastening them to it with sealing wax. The tapers cast a pale light, almost absorbed by the dead walls, their feeble flicker scarcely reaching the rest of the room; it cast its beams only upon the Holy Instruments, as it were, a ray of light falling from heaven upon the naked altar. The floor was reeking with damp. The roof sloped rapidly on both sides like the roof of the other garret, and was scored with cracks through which came the icy blast. Nothing could have been less stately, yet nothing was more solemn than this mournful ceremony. Profound silence, through which the least sound arising from la route d'Allemagne could be heard, cast a veil of somber majesty over the midnight scene. Indeed the grandeur of the action contrasted strongly with the poverty of the instruments; therefrom arose a feeling of religious awe. On each side of the altar, regardless of the deadly damp, knelt the two aged nuns upon the tiling of the floor, and prayed together with the priest. Clad in his sacrificial vestments, he set out a golden chalice adorned with precious stones, no doubt one of the sacred vessels saved from the pillage of the Abbaye de Chelles. By the side of this ciborium, recalling by

its richness the splendor of the monarchy, were placed
two glasses, scarcely good enough for the lowest inn,
containing the water and the wine for the Holy Sacrifice. For want of a missal the priest had placed his
breviary upon the corner of the altar. A common
towel was put ready for the washing of the innocent
and bloodless hands. The whole was infinite yet little;
poor but noble; at once holy and profane. The stranger
came and knelt down devoutly between the two nuns.
The priest had tied a piece of crape around the chalice
and the crucifix; having no other means of showing
the intention of this requiem mass, he had put God
Himself in mourning weeds. Suddenly the man noticed it; he was seized with a memory that held such
power over him, that the sweat stood in drops upon
his wide and lofty brow. The four silent actors of
this scene looked at one another mysteriously. Then
their souls, rising with one another in their mutual influence, communicated one to another their own sensations, and were melted together in religious pity. It
seemed as if their thought had called up the martyr
whose remains had been devoured by quicklime, and
that his shadow rose before them in all its royal majesty. They were celebrating an *obit* without the body
of the dead. Under these gaping laths and tiles four
Christians were about to intercede before God for a
King of France, were about to celebrate his funeral
without the coffin. Here was the purest of all devotion,
an astonishing act of fidelity performed without one
thought for the future. Doubtless to the eyes of God,
it was as the glass of water which weighs in the bal-
ance as heavy as the greatest virtues. The whole monarchy was present in the prayers of a priest and two

poor women; perhaps, too, the Revolution itself was represented in the man, for his face betrayed too much remorse not to cause the belief that he was fulfilling the vows of a boundless repentance.

Instead of pronouncing the Latin words, *Introibo ad altare Dei,* etc., the priest, by some divine inspiration, looked upon the three assistants—the symbols there of of Christian France—and said to them, as though to blot out the wretchedness of the garret: "We are about to enter into the Sanctuary of God!" At these words, uttered with thrilling earnestness, the server and the two nuns were filled with religious awe. God would not have revealed Himself in greater majesty under the vaults of Saint Peter at Rome, than He revealed Himself then to the eyes of these Christians in this refuge of poverty. The truth is so perfect—that between Him and man every intermediary seems useless, and that He draws His greatness only from Himself. The stranger's devotion was real, the sentiment too which united the prayers of these four servants of God and the King was unanimous. The holy words rang through the silence like heavenly music. There was a moment when the stranger was overcome with tears; it was at the *Pater Noster.* The priest added, in Latin, this petition, which the man no doubt understood: *Et remitte scelus regicidis sicut Ludovicius eis remisit semetipse.* (And forgive the regicides as Louis himself forgave them.) The two nuns saw two great tears roll down the stranger's manly cheeks and fall upon the floor. The priest recited the Office for the Dead. The *Domine salvum fac regem* intoned in a low voice, went to the hearts of the faithful Royalists when they remembered that the child-king, for whom their prayers ascended to the Most High, at that moment was a captive in the hands of his enemies. The stranger shivered at the thought that a new crime might still be committed, wherein he would no doubt be forced to take part. When the funeral service was over, the priest made a sign to the two nuns, and they went out. As soon as he found himself alone with the stranger he went up to him with a sad and gentle air, and said in a fatherly voice: "My son, if you have stained your hands in the blood of the martyr-king, confide in me. There is no sin which cannot be effaced in the eyes of God by repentance as touching and sincere as yours seems to be."

At the first words pronounced by the ecclesiastic the stranger let a movement of involuntary terror escape him; but his face recovered its calmness and he looked at the astonished priest with confidence.

"Father," said he in a voice visibly affected, "no one is more innocent than I of the blood shed——"

"I must believe you," said the priest. He paused while he once more scrutinized his penitent; then, persisting in the belief that he was one of those timorous *Conventionnels* who betrayed an inviolable and consecrated head in order to save their own, he replied in a grave voice: "Consider, my son, the fact that you have not co-operated in so great a crime is not sufficient to be absolved from it. Those men who were able to defend the King, and left their swords in their scabbards, will have a very heavy account to render to the King of Heaven. Oh! yes," continued the old priest, shaking his head impressively from right to left—"yes, very heavy!—for, by remaining aloof, they became the passive accomplices of this terrible crime!"

"You think," asked the stranger in amazement, "that indirect participation will be punished? The soldier commanded to fall into line—is he then responsible?"

The priest hesitated.

The stranger was glad of the embarrassment into which he had thrown this puritan Royalist, by placing him between the dogma of passive obedience—which, according to the Monarchists, was the essence of all military law—and the equally important dogma which magnifies into sanctity the respect due to the royal person; in the priest's silence he eagerly descried a solution to the doubts which tormented him. Then, in order not to leave the venerable *jansenist* time for further reflection, he said to him: "I should blush to offer you any fee for the funeral service you have just celebrated for the repose of the King's soul and the relief of my conscience; one cannot pay for a thing of inestimable value except by an offering also above price. Will you deign, Monsieur, to accept the gift of a holy relic which I offer you? The day will come, perhaps, when you will understand its value."

As the stranger finished these words he presented the ecclesiastic with a little box, which felt extremely light. He took it, as it were, unconsciously, for the man's solemn words, the tone in which he spoke, and the respect with which he held out the box, struck him with the profoundest astonishment. Then they returned into the room where the two nuns were waiting.

"You are in a house," said the stranger, "belonging to a man—Mucius Scaevola, the plasterer, who lives on the first floor—who is well known in the section for his patriotism; but he is secretly attached to the Bour-

bons. He was formerly huntsman to Monseigneur le
Prince de Conti, and owes all his fortune to him. As
long as you do not go out of his house, you are safer
than any other place in France. Stay here; there are
pious souls who will watch over your wants, and you
will be able to wait, without danger, for less evil times.
In a year, on the 21st of January"—(as he pronounced
these last words he could not hide an involuntary shudder)—"if you do adopt this wretched place for your
refuge, I will return to celebrate the expiatory mass
with you——"

He did not finish his sentence. Then, saluting the
silent inhabitants of the attic, he cast a last look on
all the signs of their poverty and disappeared.

For the two innocent nuns, such an adventure assumed all the interest of a romance. As soon, then, as
the venerable Abbé had informed them of the mysterious gift which the man had made him, so solemnly,
they placed the box on the table, and their three anxious
faces, faintly lit up by the light of a tallow dip, betrayed an indescribable curiosity. Mademoiselle de
Langeais opened the box, and found a very fine *batiste*
handkerchief, soiled with sweat; when they unfolded it
they found that there were stains upon it.

"It is blood!" said the priest.

"It is marked with the royal crown!" exclaimed the
other sister.

The two nuns dropped the precious relic in horror.
For these two simple souls the mystery which enveloped the stranger became inexplicable; as to the priest,
from that day he did not even attempt to account for
it.

The three prisoners soon perceived, in spite of the

Terror, that a powerful hand was stretched out over them. First, they received provisions and fuel; then, the two nuns discovered that there must be a woman co-operating with their protector, for linen and clothes were sent them which enabled them to go out without exciting remark by the aristocratic fashion of the dresses which they had been obliged to continue to wear; finally, Mucius Scaevola gave them two *cartes civiques*. From time to time warnings necessary to the safety of the priest reached them in roundabout ways. These counsels came so opportunely that they were convinced they could only have been given by a person initiated into secrets of State. In spite of the famine which weighed over Paris, these outlaws found rations of white bread regularly brought to the door of their cabin by invisible hands; however, they thought they had discovered in Mucius Scaevola the mysterious agent of these benefactions, which were always both suitably timed and ingeniously carried out. The three nobles then, who continued to dwell in the same attic, could not doubt that their protector was the person who had come to celebrate the mass of expiation during the night of the 22nd of January, 1793; thus he became the object of their special devotion; he was their only hope, they lived through him alone. They had added to their prayers special prayers for him; night and morning the pious creatures offered their vows for his happiness, prosperity, and safety; they besought God to keep far from him every snare, to deliver him from his enemies and grant him a long and peaceful life. To their gratitude, renewed so to speak every day, was necessarily allied a feeling of curiosity which grew each day more intense. The cir-

cumstances that had attended the stranger's appari-
tion were the subject of their conversations; they
formed a thousand conjectures concerning him; even
the mere distraction of thought which he caused was
a fresh source of advantage to them. They promised
themselves to make sure of not letting him escape from
their gratitude the evening he would come back, according to his promise, to celebrate the sad anniversary
of the death of Louis XVI. That night, so impatiently awaited, arrived at last. At midnight, the
sound of the stranger's heavy footsteps was heard
upon the old wooden staircase; the room had been prepared to receive him, the altar was vested. This time
the sisters opened the door to greet him, and both hastened to the stairs with a light. Mademoiselle de
Langeais even went a few steps down in order to see
their benefactor the sooner.

"Come," she said kindly, in a voice broken by emotion—"come, we were expecting you."

The man raised his head, cast a somber look at the
nun, and made no answer. She felt as if a mantle of
ice had fallen upon her; she was silent. Gratitude and
curiosity expired in their hearts at the sight of him.
Perhaps he seemed to them, whose hearts were excited
by sentiment and disposed to expand into friendship,
more chilling, taciturn, and terrible than he really was.
The three poor prisoners comprehended that he desired to remain a stranger to them, and resigned themselves. The priest fancied he saw a smile upon the man's
lips at the moment he perceived the preparation that
they had made for his reception; but he immediately re-
pressed it. He heard mass and prayed, then he departed,
after having replied with a few polite words of refusal

to Mademoiselle de Langeais's invitation to partake of the little collation which they had prepared.

After the 9th of *Thermidor,* the nuns and the Abbé de Marolles were able to walk through Paris without the least risk. The first expedition which the Abbé made was to a perfumery shop, at the sign of *La Reine des fleurs,* kept by a *citoyen* and *citoyenne* Ragon, late perfumers to the Court, who remained faithful to the royal family, and whom the Vendéans made use of to correspond with the Princes and the Royalist Committee in Paris. The Abbé, dressed as the times required, was just at the doorstep of this shop, which was situated between Saint Roche and la rue des Trondeurs —when a crowd that filled la rue Saint Honoré prevented his going out.

"What's this?" said he to Madame Ragon.

"It is nothing," she replied; "only the tumbril and the executioner going to la Place Louis XV. Ah! we saw it often enough last year; but to-day, just four days after the anniversary of the Twenty-first of January, one can look at the ghastly procession without any pain."

"Why," said the Abbé, "what you say is not Christian."

"Ah! but it is the execution of Robespierre's accomplices. They defended themselves as long as they could, but now it's their turn—over there, where they have sent so many innocent men."

The crowd filled la rue Saint Honoré, and passed by like a flood. The Abbé de Marolles, yielding to an impulse of curiosity, looked, and saw above the heads of the crowd, standing erect on the tumbril, the man who had heard his Mass three days before.

"Who is it?" said he; "the man——"

"It's the executioner," answered Monsieur Ragon, calling the *exécuteur des hautes œuvres* by his title under the monarchy.

"*Mon ami, mon ami!*" cried Madame Ragon; "Monsieur d'Abbé is dying!" and the old lady got a flask of vinegar to bring the priest to his senses, for he had fainted. "No doubt what he gave me," said he, "was the handkerchief with which the King wiped his face when he was going to his martyrdom.—Poor man! The axe had a heart in its steel when none was found in all France!"

The perfumers thought the poor priest was delirious.

MADAME DE DEY'S LAST RECEPTION

MADAME DE DEY'S LAST RECEPTION

"Sometimes they saw that by some phenomenon of Vision or
Locomotion he could abolish Space in both its moods—Time and
Distance—whereof the one is intellectual and the other physical."
—Louis Lambart.

ONE evening in the month of November, 1793, the
principal inhabitants of Carentan were collected in
the *salon* of Madame de Dey, who held an *Assembly*
every evening. Certain circumstances which would
have attracted no notice in a large town, but were such
as to mightily interest a small one, imparted a peculiar
importance to this customary gathering. Two days before, Madame de Dey had closed her doors to her
visitors on the ground of indisposition, and had also
announced that she would be unable to receive them
the following evening. At an ordinary time these two
events would have produced the same effect at Carentan as a *relache* at all the theaters produces in Paris;
on these days, existence seems in a sense incomplete.
But in 1793, the action of Madame de Dey was one
which might lead to the most disastrous consequences.
At that time, a step involving a noble in the least risk
was nearly always a matter of life and death. In order
to understand properly the keen curiosity and petty

craftiness which on that evening animated the faces of all these respectable Normans; and still more, in order to share the secret perplexities of Madame de Dey, it is necessary to explain the part she played at Carentan. As the critical position in which she was situated at this time was no doubt the position of many during the Revolution, the sympathies of not a few of my readers will add their own color to this narrative.

Madame de Dey was the widow of a Lieutenant General decorated with several orders. At the beginning of the Emigration she had left the Court, and as she owned considerable property in the neighborhood of Carentan, she had taken refuge there, in the hope that the influence of the Terror would make itself felt in those parts. This supposition, founded on an exact knowledge of the country, proved correct, for the ravages of the Revolution in Lower Normandy were slight. Although, formerly, when she came to visit her property she had only associated with the local *noblesse,* now, out of policy, she opened her doors to the principal townspeople and the new authorities of Carentan, exerting herself to flatter them by the compliment of her acquaintance, and at the same time to avoid awakening their hatred or their jealousy. Kind and courteous, gifted with an indescribable sweetness of manner, she knew how to please without recourse to cringing or entreaty, and had thus succeeded in winning general esteem. This was due to her exquisite tact, which by its sage promptings enabled her to steer a difficult course and satisfy the exigencies of a mixed society; she neither humiliated the tetchy self-conceit of the parvenus nor shocked the sensibilities of her old friends.

At the age of about thirty-eight, she still preserved —not that fresh buxom beauty which distinguishes the girls of Lower Normandy—but a slender, so to speak, aristocratic type. Her features were delicately chiselled and her figure pliant and graceful; when she spoke, her pale face seemed to light up with fresh life. Her large dark eyes were full of kindly courtesy, but an expression of religious calm within them seemed to show that the principle of her existence lay no longer in herself. She had been married at an early age to an old and jealous soldier, and the falseness of her position in the midst of a dissolute court, had no doubt done much to spread a veil of grave melancholy over a face which must once have beamed with all the charm and vivacity of Love. Obliged to repress unceasingly the instinctive impulses and emotions of woman, at a time when she still feels rather than reflects, with her, passion had remained virgin in the depth of her heart. Thus her chief attraction was derived from this inward youthfulness, which betrayed itself at certain moments in her countenance, and gave her ideas an innocent expression of desire. Her appearance commanded respect, but in her manner and her voice, impulses toward an unknown future such as spring in the heart of a young girl, were continually showing themselves. The least susceptible men soon found themselves in love with her, and yet were impressed with a sort of fear of her, inspired by her courtly bearing. Her soul, great by nature but rendered strong by cruel struggles, seemed to be raised too high for common humanity, and of this men appeared to be conscious. To such a soul, a lofty passion is a necessity.

Thus all Madame de Dey's affections were concentrated in one single sentiment—the sentiment of Maternity. The happiness and pleasures of which she had been deprived as a wife she found again in the intense love she bore her son. She loved him, not only with the pure and deep devotion of a mother, but with the coquetry of a mistress and the jealousy of a wife. She was miserable when he was far from her, anxious when he had gone out; she could never see enough of him; she lived only in him and for him. To give an idea of the strength of this sentiment in Madame de Dey, it will be enough to add that this son, besides being her only child, was the last relation left her, the only creature on whom she could fasten the hopes and fears and joys of her life. The late Count was the last of his family, and the Countess the sole heiress of hers, so that every worldly calculation and interest combined with the noblest needs of the soul to intensify in her heart a sentiment already so strong in the heart of woman. It was only by infinite care that she had succeeded in rearing her son, and this had endeared him still more to her. 'The doctor had pronounced twenty times over that she must lose him, but she was confident in her own hopes and presentiments. So in spite of the decrees of the Faculty, she had the inexpressible joy of seeing him pass safely through the perils of infancy, and then of watching with wonder the continued improvement of his health.

Thanks to her constant care, her son had grown into a young man of so much promise that at the age of twenty he was looked upon as one of the most accomplished gentlemen at the Court of Versailles. Above all, happy in a crown unattained by the efforts of every mother, she was adored by her son; they understood one another, heart to heart, in fraternal sympathy. If they had not been already bound together by the bonds of nature, they would have instinctively felt for each other that mutual friendship between men which is so rarely met with in life.

The young Count had been appointed sub-lieutenant at the age of eighteen, and in obedience to the code of honor of the day had followed the princes in their Emigration.

Thus it was impossible for Madame de Dey, being noble, rich, and the mother of an Emigrant, to hide from herself the dangers of her cruel situation. With no other aim than to save her large fortune for her son, she had given up the happiness of accompanying him; but when she read at Carentan the stringent laws under which the Republic was confiscating every day the property of Emigrants, she exulted in her act of courage, for was she not preserving her son's wealth at the risk of her own life? Later on, when she heard of the terrible executions decreed by the Convention, she slept in peace, knowing that her only treasure was in safety, far from danger and the scaffold. She congratulated herself in the belief that she had taken the best means of preserving both her treasures at once. By consecrating to this secret thought the concessions which those unhappy times demanded, she neither compromised her womanly dignity nor her aristocratic convictions, but hid her sorrows under a cold veil of mystery.

She had grasped all the difficulties which awaited her at Carentan. To come there and fill the first place was in itself a daily tempting of the scaffold. But supported by her mothérly courage, she was enabled to win the affection of the poor by consoling the misery of all without distinction, and to make herself indispensable to the rich by ministering to their pleasures.

She entertained at her house the *Procureur* of the Commune, the Mayor, the President of the district, the Public Prosecutor, and even the judges of the Revolutionary Court. Of these personages the first four were unmarried, and paid their addresses to her. Each of them hoped she would marry him, either from fear of the harm that it was in their power to do her, or for the sake of the protection which they had to offer her. The Public Prosecutor, formerly an attorney at Caèn, employed to manage the Countess's business, adopted an artifice which was most dangerous for her. He tried a generous and devoted line of conduct, in the hope of inspiring her with affection. In this way he was the most formidable of all her suitors, and as she had formerly been a client of his, he alone knew intimately the condition and extent of her fortune. His passion was therefore reinforced by all the desires of avarice, and further supported by immense power— the power of life and death over the whole district. This man, who was still young, proceeded with so fine a show of generosity that Madame de Dey had not as yet been able to form a true estimate of him. But despite the danger of a trial of craft with Normans, she made use of all the inventive wit and duplicity bestowed by nature on women, to play off these rivals one against the other. By gaining time, she hoped to reach the end of her difficulties, safe and sound. At this period the royalists of the interior went on flattering themselves from day to day that on the morrow they would see the end of the Republic; it was this persuasion which brought many of them to ruin.

In spite of these difficulties, by the exercise of considerable address, the Countess had maintained her independence up to the day on which she had determined, with unaccountable imprudence, to close her doors to her guests. She inspired such a real and deep interest, that the people who had come to her house that evening were seriously perturbed when they heard it was impossible for her to receive them. Then, with that barefaced curiosity which is ingrained in provincial manners, they immediately began to make inquiries as to what trouble, or annoyance, or illness, she suffered from. To these questions an old housekeeper named Brigitte answered, that her mistress kept her room and would see no one, not even the members of her household.

The semi-claustral life led by the inhabitants of a small town forms a habit of analyzing and explaining the actions of others, so germane to them as to become invincible. So after having pitied Madame de Dey, without really knowing whether she was happy or unhappy, each one set himself to discover the cause of her sudden retirement.

"If she were ill," said the first inquisitor, "she would have sent for advice; but the doctor has been at my house the whole day playing chess. He was joking with me and saying that there is only one disease nowadays . . . and that's incurable."

This jest was hazarded with caution.

Men and women, old and young, set themselves to scour the vast field of conjecture; each one thought

he spied a secret, and this secret occupied all their
imaginations.

By the next day their suspicions had grown more
venomous. As life in a small town is balanced up to
date, the women learned, the first thing in the morning, that Brigitte had made larger purchases at the
market than usual. This was an indisputable fact.
Brigitte had been seen very early in the *Place,* and—
marvelous to relate!—she had bought the only hare
there was to be got. Now the whole town knew that
Madame de Dey did not care for game, so this hare
became the object of endless speculation. Then, as
the old men were taking their usual stroll, they observed a sort of concentrated activity in the Countess's
house, betrayed by the very precautions that the servants took to conceal it. The valet was beating a carpet
in the garden; the evening before no one would have
noticed it, but as every one was constructing a romance
of his own, this carpet served them for a foundation.
Each person had a different tale.

The second day, the principal personages of Carentan, hearing that Madame de Dey announced that she
was unwell, met for the evening at the house of the
Mayor's brother, a retired merchant. He was a married man, honorable, and generally respected, the
Countess herself having a great regard for him. On
this occasion all the aspirants to the rich widow's hand
had a more or less probable story to tell, while each of
them pondered how to turn to his own profit the secret
which obliged her to compromise herself in the way
she had. The Public Prosecutor imagined all the details of a drama in which her son was to be brought to
the Countess by night. The Mayor believed that a

priest who had refused the oaths had come from La
Vendée, and sought refuge. The President of the district was convinced it was a Chouan or Vendéan
leader, hotly pursued. Others inclined to a noble escaped from the prisons in Paris. In short, everybody
suspected that the Countess had been guilty of one
of those acts of generosity, denominated by the laws
of that time "crimes," and such as might bring her to
the scaffold. However, the Public Prosecutor whispered that they must be silent, and try to save the unfortunate lady from the abyss into which she was
hurrying.

"If you publish this affair abroad," he added, "I
shall be obliged to interfere, search her house, and
then——!" He said no more, but every one understood his reticence.

The Countess's true friends were so much alarmed
for her, that, on the morning of the third day, the
Procureur Syndic of the Commune got his wife to
write her a note, entreating her to hold her reception
that evening as usual. The old merchant, bolder still,
presented himself during the morning at Madame de
Dey's house. Confident in his desire to serve her, he
insisted on being shown in, when to his utter amazement he caught sight of her in the garden, engaged in
cutting the last flowers in her borders to fill her vases.

"There's no doubt she has given refuge to her
lover," said the old man, struck with pity for this
charming woman. The strange expression of her face
confirmed his suspicions. Deeply moved by a devotion
natural in woman but always touching to us—because
every man is flattered by the sacrifices a woman makes
for one of them—the merchant informed the Countess

of the reports which were going about the town, and
of the danger she was in. "For," he concluded, "if
certain of our functionaries would not be disinclined
to pardon your heroism, if a priest were the object, no
one will have any pity on you, if it is discovered that
you are sacrificing yourself to the dictates of the
heart."

At these words Madame de Dey looked at him in
such a strange, wild way, that, old man as he was, he
could not help shuddering.

"Come," said she, taking him by the hand and leading him into her own room. After making sure that
they were alone, she drew from her bosom a soiled and
crumpled letter.

"Read it," she cried, pronouncing the words with a
violent effort.

She fell back into her easy chair completely overcome. While the old merchant was looking for his
spectacles and wiping them clean, she raised her eyes to
his face, and for the first time gazed at him curiously;
then she said sweetly, and in a changed voice: "I can
trust you."

"Am I not going to take a share in your crime?" answered the worthy man simply.

She shuddered. For the first time in that little
town her soul found sympathy in the soul of another.
The old merchant understood immediately both the de-
jection and the joy of the Countess. Her son had
taken part in the expedition of Granville, he had written to his mother from the depth of his prison to give
her one sad, sweet hope. Confident in his plan of
escape, he named three days within which he would
present himself at her house in disguise. The fatal

letter contained heartrending *adieux* in case he should
not be at Carentan by the evening of the third day. He
also entreated his mother to remit a considerable sum
of money to the messenger who had undertaken to
carry this missive to her, through innumerable dangers.

The paper quivered in the old man's hands.

"And this is the third day," cried Madame de Dey.

Then she rose hastily, took the letter, and began to
walk up and down the room.

"You have not been altogether prudent," said the
merchant. "Why did you have provisions got in?"

"But he may arrive dying with hunger, worn out
with fatigue, and——" She could not go on.

"I am certain of my brother," answered the old
man; "I will go and get him on your side."

The merchant summoned up all the keenness which
he had formerly employed in his commercial affairs.
He gave the Countess the most prudent and sagacious
directions, and after having agreed together as to
everything they both were to say and do, the old man
invented a plausible pretext for visiting all the principal houses of Carentan. He announced in each that
he had just seen Madame de Dey, and that she would
hold her reception that evening, in spite of her indisposition. In the cross-examination which each family
subjected him to on the nature of the Countess's
malady, his keenness was a match for the shrewd Normans. He managed to start on the wrong track almost every one who busied themselves with this mysterious affair. His first visit did wonders; it was to
an old lady who suffered from gout. To her he related that Madame de Dey had almost died from an
attack of gout on the stomach, and went on to say that

the famous Tronchin having formerly prescribed, on a similar occasion, the skin of a hare flayed alive to be laid on the chest, and for the patient to lie in bed without stirring; the Countess, who was in imminent danger two days before, after having scrupulously carried out Tronchin's extraordinary prescription, now felt sufficiently convalescent to receive any one who liked to visit her that evening. This tale had an enormous success, and the doctor of Carentan, himself a royalist *in petto,* increased its effect by the earnestness with which he discussed the remedy. However, suspicion had taken too deep root in the minds of certain obstinate or philosophic persons to be entirely dissipated; so that evening the guests of Madame de Dey were eager to arrive at her house at an early hour, some to spy into her face, some out of friendship, and most from astonishment at her marvelous cure. They found the Countess sitting in her salon at the corner of the large chimney-piece.

Her room was almost as severe as the salons of Carentan, for, to avoid wounding her narrow-minded guests, she had denied herself the pleasures of luxury to which she had been accustomed before, and had made no changes in her house. The floor of the reception-room was not even polished; she let the old dingy stuffs still hang upon the walls, still kept the country furniture, burned tallow candles, and in fact followed the fashions of Carentan. She had adopted provincial life without shrinking from its cruellest pettiness or its most disagreeable privations. But knowing that her guests would pardon her any expenditure conducive to their own comfort, she neglected nothing which could afford them personal enjoyment; at her house they were always sure of an excellent dinner. She even went so far as to feign avarice to please their calculating minds, and led them on to disapprove of certain details as concessions to luxury, in order to show that she could yield with grace.

Toward seven o'clock in the evening the upper middle-class society of Carentan was assembled at her house, and formed a large circle round her hearth. The mistress of the house, supported in her trouble by the old merchant's compassionate glances, submitted with unheard-of courage to the minute questionings and stupid, frivolous talk of her guests. But at every rap of the knocker, and whenever a footstep sounded in the street, she could scarcely control her emotion. She raised discussions affecting the prosperity of the district and such burning questions as the quality of ciders, and was so well seconded by her confidant that the company almost forgot to spy upon her, the expression of her face was so natural and her assurance so imperturbable. However, the Public Prosecutor and one of the Judges of the Revolutionary Tribunal kept silence, watching attentively the least movement of her features, and listening, in spite of the noise, to every sound in the house. Every now and then they would ask some question calculated to embarrass her, but these she answered with admirable presence of mind. She proved how great a mother's courage can be.

After having arranged the card tables and settled every one to *boston*, or *reversi*, or *whist*, Madame de Dey still remained talking with the greatest nonchalance to some young people; she played her part like a consummate actress. Presently she led them on to ask for *loto*, pretended to be the only person who knew where it was, and left the room.

"Ma pauvre Brigitte," she cried, "I feel almost suffocated."

Her eyes were brilliant with fever and grief and impatience as she dried the tears which started quickly from them. "He is not coming," she said, looking into the bedroom into which she had come. "Here I can breathe and live. But in a few minutes more he will be here! for he is alive, I am certain he is alive. My heart tells me so. Do you not hear something, Brigitte? Oh! I would give the rest of my life to know whether he is in prison or walking across the country. I would give anything not to think."

She looked around once again to see if everything was in order in the room. A good fire burned brightly in the grate, the shutters were shut close, the furniture was polished until it shone again; the very way in which the bed was made was enough to prove that the Countess herself as well as Brigitte had been busy about the smallest details. Her hopes too were manifest in all the delicate care that had evidently been spent upon this room. The scent of the flowers she had placed there seemed to shed forth, mingled with their own perfume, the gracious sweetness and the chastest caresses of love. Only a mother could thus have anticipated a soldier's wants, and prepared him such complete satisfaction of them. A dainty meal, choice wines, slippers, clean linen—in short, everything necessary or agreeable to a weary traveler, were collected together, that he might want for nothing, and that the delights of home might remind him of a mother's love.

The Countess went and placed a seat at the table as /
if to realize her prayers and increase the strength of
her illusions. As she did so she cried in a heartrending voice, "Brigitte !"

"Ah, Madame, he will come; he cannot be far off.
I am certain that he is alive and on the way," replied
Brigitte. "I put a key in the Bible, and rested it on
my fingers, while Cottin read the Gospel of St. John—
and, Madame, the key did not turn."

"Is that a sure sign?" asked the Countess.

"Oh, Madame, it's well known; I would stake my
soul that he is still alive. God would never deceive us
like that."

"In spite of the danger he will be in here; still, I
long to see him."

"Poor Monsieur Auguste," cried Brigitte, "no doubt
he is on the roads, on foot."

"Hark, that is eight striking," exclaimed the Countess in terror.

She was afraid that she had stayed too long in the
room, but there she could believe that her son still
lived when she saw everything bear witness to his life.
She went downstairs, but before going into the salon
she waited a moment under the colonnade of the staircase, and listened for some sound to awaken the silent
echoes of the town. She smiled at Brigitte's husband,
who kept watch like a sentinel; his eyes seemed stupefied with straining to catch the murmurs of the *Place*
and the first sounds of the night. Everywhere and
in everything she saw her son.

A moment afterward she had returned to her guests,
affecting an air of gaiety, and sat down to play at *loto*
with some girls. But every now and then she com-

plained of feeling unwell, and went to recline in her easy chair by the fireplace.

Such was the situation, material and mental, in the house of Madame de Dey. Meanwhile, on the high road from Paris to Cherbourg, a young man clad in a brown *carmagnole,* a costume in vogue at this period, directed his steps toward Carentan.

In the commencement of the *Réquisitions* there was little or no discipline. The exigencies of the moment scarcely allowed the Republic to equip its soldiers fully at once, so that it was nothing unusual to see the roads full of *réquisitionnaires* still wearing their civil clothes. These young men arrived at the halting-places before their battalions or remained there behind them, for the progress of each man depended on his personal capability of enduring the fatigues of a long journey. The traveler in question found himself considerably in advance of a battalion of *réquisitionnaires* which was on its way to Cherbourg, and which the Mayor of Carentan was waiting for from hour to hour to billet on the inhabitants. The young man walked with heavy steps, but still he did not falter, and his gait seemed to show that he had long been accustomed to the severities of military life. Though the moon shed her light upon the pastures around Carentan, he had noticed a thick white bank of clouds ready to cover the whole country with snow. The fear of being caught in a hurricane no doubt hastened his steps, for he was walking at a pace little suited to his weariness. He carried an almost empty knapsack on his back and in his hand a boxwood stick, cut from one of the high thick hedges which this shrub forms round most of the estates of Lower Normandy.

The towers of Carentan, thrown into fantastic relief by the moonlight, had only just come into sight, when this solitary traveler entered the town. His footfall awakened the echoes of the silent streets. He did not meet a creature, so he was obliged to inquire for the house of the Mayor from a weaver who was still at his work. The Mayor lived only a short distance off, and the *réquisitionnaire* soon found himself under shelter in the porch of his house. Here he applied for a billet order and sat down on a stone seat to wait. However, the Mayor sent for him, so he was obliged to appear before him and become the object of a scrupulous examination. The *réquisitionnaire* was a foot soldier, a young man of fine bearing, apparently belonging to a family of distinction. His manners had the air of gentle birth, and his face expressed all the intelligence due to a good education.

"What is your name?" asked the Mayor, casting a knowing glance at him.

"Julien Jussieu," replied the *réquisitionnaire*.

The magistrate let an incredulous smile escape him.

"And you come——"

"From Paris."

"Your comrades must be some distance off," replied the Norman in a bantering tone.

"I am three leagues in front of the battalion."

"No doubt some sentiment draws you to Carentan, *citoyen réquisitionnaire?*" said the Mayor with a shrewd look. "It is all right," he continued. The young man was about to speak, but he motioned him to be silent and went on, "You can go, *Citoyen Jussieu!*"

There was a tinge of irony discernible in his accent,

as he pronounced these two last words and held out to him a billet order which directed him to the house of Madame de Dey. The young man read the address with an air of curiosity.

"He knows well enough that he hasn't got far to go; when he's once outside he won't be long crossing the *Place!*" exclaimed the Mayor, talking to himself as the young man went out. "He's a fine bold fellow; God help him! He's got an answer ready to every-thing. Ay, but if it had been any one else but me, and they had demanded to see his papers—it would have been all up with him."

At this moment the clocks of Carentan struck half-past nine. In the antechamber at Madame de Dey's the lanterns were lighted, the servants were helping their masters and mistresses to put on their clogs and *houppelandes* and mantles, the card players had settled their accounts, and they were all leaving together, ac-cording to the established custom in little towns.

When they had exhausted all the formularies of adieu and were separating in the *Place,* each in the direction of his own house, one of the ladies, observing that that important personage was not with them, re-marked, "It appears that the Prosecutor intends to re-main."

As a matter of fact, the Countess was at that moment alone with that terrible magistrate; she waited, trembling, till it should please him to depart.

After a long silence, which inspired her with a feel-ing of terror, he said at last, "*Citoyenne,* I am here to carry out the laws of the Republic."

Madame de Dey shuddered.

"Hast thou nothing to reveal to me?" he asked.

"Nothing," she replied, in astonishment.

"Ah, Madame," cried the Prosecutor, sitting down beside her and changing his tone, "at this moment one word could send us—you and me—to the scaffold. I have watched your character, your mind, your manners too closely to share in the mystification by which you have succeeded in misleading your guests this evening. You are expecting your son, I have not the least doubt of it."

The Countess made an involuntary gesture of denial; but she had grown pale, the muscles of her face had contracted under the necessity of displaying a coolness she did not feel; the pitiless eye of the Prosecutor had not lost one of these movements.

"Well, receive him," replied this magistrate of the Revolution, "but do not let him remain under your roof after seven o'clock in the morning. Tomorrow at daybreak I shall come to your house armed with a denunciation which I shall get drawn up."

She looked at him with a bewildered, numbed look that might have drawn pity from a tiger.

"I shall demonstrate," he continued sweetly, "the falsity of this denunciation by a careful search. You will then be screened by the nature of my report from all ulterior suspicions. I shall speak of your patriotic gifts, your *civism*, and we shall be saved."

Madame de Dey suspected a snare; she remained motionless, her tongue was frozen and her face on fire. The sound of the knocker echoed through the house.

"Ah," cried the mother as she fell in terror upon her knees, "save him! save him!"

The Public Prosecutor cast a passionate glance at her.

"Yes, let us save him," he replied, "even at the cost of our own lives." He raised her politely.

"I am lost," she cried.

'Ah, Madame!" he answered, with an oratorical gesture, "I would not owe you to anything—but to yourself alone."

"Madame, he's——" cried Brigitte, thinking her mistress was alone.

At the sight of the Public Prosecutor, the old servant, who had burst in, beaming with joy, grew pale and motionless.

"Who is it, Brigitte?" asked the magistrate, with an air of gentle intelligence.

"A *réquisitionnaire* sent us from the Mayor's to lodge," answered the servant, showing him the billet order. The Prosecutor read the paper. "True,'' said he; "a battalion is coming to us to-night." He went out.

At that moment the Countess had too much need to believe in the sincerity of her former attorney for the least doubt of it to cross her mind!

Though she had scarcely the power to stand, she ascended the staircase precipitately, opened the door of the room, saw her son, and threw herself half dead into his arms. "My child, my child," she sobbed, almost beside herself, as she covered him with kisses.

"Madame!" said a stranger's voice.

"Ah, it is not he!" she cried, recoiling in horror. She stood upright before the *réquisitionnaire* and gazed at him with haggard eyes. "My good God, how like he is!" said Brigitte. There was a moment's silence; even the stranger shuddered at the sight of Madame de Dey.

The first blow had almost killed her, and now she felt the full extent of her grief. She leaned for support on Brigitte's husband. "Ah, Monsieur," she said, "I could not bear to see you any longer. Allow me to leave you for my servants to entertain."

She went down to her own room, half carried by Brigitte and her old man-servant. "What! Madame," cried the housekeeper, as she led her mistress to a chair; "is that man going to sleep in Monsieur Auguste's bed, and wear Monsieur Auguste's slippers, and eat the pastry that I made for Monsieur Auguste? If I was to be guillotined for it, I——"

"Brigitte!" cried Madame de Dey.

Brigitte was mute.

"Hold thy tongue, chatterbox," said her husband in a low voice. "Dost want to kill Madame?"

At this moment the *réquisitionnaire* made a noise in his room as he sat down to the table.

"I cannot stay here," cried Madame de Dey. "I will go into the conservatory; I shall be able to hear better there what goes on outside during the night."

She was still tossed between the fear of having lost her son and the hope of seeing him come back to her.

The silence of the night was horrible. The arrival of the battalion of *réquisitionnaires* in the town when each man sought his lodging, was a terrible moment for the Countess. Her hopes were cheated at every footfall, at every sound; presently nature resumed her awful calm.

Toward morning the Countess was obliged to return to her own room.

Brigitte, who was watching her mistress's movements, not seeing her come out, went into the room and found the Countess dead.

"She must have heard that *réquisitionnaire*," cried Brigitte. "As soon as he has finished dressing, there he is, marching up and down Monsieur Auguste's bedroom, as if he were in a stable, singing their damned *Marseillaise!* It was enough to kill her."

The death of the Countess was due to a deeper sentiment, and doubtless caused by some terrible vision. At the exact hour when Madame de Dey died at Carentan, her son was shot in le Morbihan.

We may add this tragic event to all the evidence of sympathies ignoring the laws of space, which has been collected through the learning and curiosity of certain recluses. These documents will some day serve as the groundwork whereon to base a new science—a science which has hitherto lacked its man of genius.

A PASSION IN THE DESERT

A PASSION IN THE DESERT

"THE whole show is dreadful," she cried, coming out of the menagerie of M. Martin. She had just been looking at that daring speculator "working with his hyena"—to speak in the style of the program.

"By what means," she continued, "can he have tamed these animals to such a point as to be certain of their affection for——"

"What seems to you a problem," said I, interrupting, "is really quite natural."

"Oh!" she cried, letting an incredulous smile wander over her lips.

"You think that beasts are wholly without passions?" I asked her. "Quite the reverse; we can communicate to them all the vices arising in our own state of civilization."

She looked at me with an air of astonishment.

"Nevertheless," I continued, "the first time I saw M. Martin, I admit, like you, I did give vent to an exclamation of surprise. I found myself next to an old soldier with the right leg amputated, who had come in with me. His face had struck me. He had one of those intrepid heads, stamped with the seal of warfare, and on which the battles of Napoleon are written. Besides, he had that frank good-humored expression which always impresses me favorably. He was with-

119

out doubt one of those troopers who are surprised at nothing, who find matter for laughter in the contortions of a dying comrade, who bury or plunder him quite light-heartedly, who stand intrepidly in the way of bullets; in fact, one of those men who waste no time in deliberation, and would not hesitate to make friends with the devil himself. After looking very attentively at the proprietor of the menagerie getting out of his box, my companion pursed up his lips with an air of mockery and contempt, with that peculiar and expressive twist which superior people assume to show they are not taken in. Then when I was expatiating on the courage of M. Martin, he smiled, shook his head knowingly, and said, 'Well known.'

" 'How "well known"?' I said. 'If you would only explain me the mystery I should be vastly obliged.'

"After a few minutes, during which we made acquaintance, we went to dine at the first *restaurateur's* whose shop caught our eye. At dessert a bottle of champagne completely refreshed and brightened up the memories of this odd old soldier. He told me his story, and I said that he had every reason to exclaim, 'Well known.' "

.   .   .   .   .   .

When she got home, she teased me to that extent, and made so many promises, that I consented to communicate to her the old soldier's confidences. Next day she received the following episode of an epic which one might call "The Frenchman in Egypt."

During the expedition in Upper Egypt under General Desaix, a Provençal soldier fell into the hands of the Mangrabins, and was taken by these Arabs into the deserts beyond the falls of the Nile.

In order to place a sufficient distance between themselves and the French army, the Mangrabins made forced marches, and only rested during the night. They camped round a well overshadowed by palm trees under which they had previously concealed a store of provisions. Not surmising that the notion of flight would occur to their prisoner, they contented themselves with binding his hands, and after eating a few dates, and giving provender to their horses, went to sleep.

When the brave Provençal saw that his enemies were no longer watching him, he made use of his teeth to steal a scimitar, fixed the blade between his knees, and cut the cords which prevented using his hands; in a moment he was free. He at once seized a rifle and a dagger, then taking the precaution to provide himself with a sack of dried dates, oats, and powder and shot, and to fasten a scimitar to his waist, he leaped onto a horse, and spurred on vigorously in the direction where he thought to find the French army. So impatient was he to see a bivouac again that he pressed on the already tired courser at such speed that its flanks were lacerated with his spurs, and at last the poor animal died, leaving the Frenchman alone in the desert. After walking some time in the sand with all the courage of an escaped convict, the soldier was obliged to stop, as the day had already ended. In spite of the beauty of an oriental sky at night, he felt he had not strength enough to go on. Fortunately he had been able to find a small hill, on the summit of which a few palm trees shot up into the air; it was their verdure seen from afar which had brought hope and consolation to his heart. His fatigue was so

great that he lay down upon a rock of granite, capriciously cut out like a camp-bed; there he fell asleep
without taking any precaution to defend himself while
he slept. He had made the sacrifice of his life. His
last thought was one of regret. He repented having
left the Mangrabins, whose nomad life seemed to smile
on him now that he was afar from them and without
help. He was awakened by the sun, whose pitiless rays
fell with all their force on the granite and produced
an intolerable heat—for he had had the stupidity to
place himself inversely to the shadow thrown by the
verdant majestic heads of the palm trees. He looked
at the solitary trees and shuddered—they reminded
him of the graceful shafts crowned with foliage which
characterize the Saracen columns in the cathedral of
Arles.

But when, after counting the palm trees, he cast his
eye around him, the most horrible despair was infused
into his soul. Before him stretched an ocean without
limit. The dark sand of the desert spread farther than
sight could reach in every direction, and glittered like
steel struck with bright light. It might have been a
sea of looking-glass, or lakes melted together in a
mirror. A fiery vapor carried up in streaks made a
perpetual whirlwind over the quivering land. The
sky was lit with an oriental splendor of insupportable
purity, leaving naught for the imagination to desire.
Heaven and earth were on fire.

The silence was awful in its wild and terrible majesty. Infinity, immensity, closed in upon the soul from
every side. Not a cloud in the sky, not a breath in the
air, not a flaw on the bosom of the sand, ever moving
in diminutive waves; the horizon ended as at sea on a

clear day, with one line of light, definite as the cut of a sword.

The Provençal threw his arms round the trunk of one of the palm trees, as though it were the body of a friend, and then in the shelter of the thin straight shadow that the palm cast upon the granite, he wept. Then sitting down he remained as he was, contemplating with profound sadness the implacable scene, which was all he had to look upon. He cried aloud, to measure the solitude. His voice, lost in the hollows of the hill, sounded faintly, and aroused no echo—the echo was in his own heart. The Provençal was twenty-two years old:—he loaded his carbine.

"There'll be time enough," he said to himself, laying on the ground the weapon which alone could bring him deliverance.

Looking by turns at the black expanse and the blue expanse, the soldier dreamed of France—he smelt with delight the gutters of Paris—he remembered the towns through which he had passed, the faces of his fellow-soldiers, the most minute details of his life. His southern fancy soon showed him the stones of his beloved Provence, in the play of the heat which waved over the spread sheet of the desert. Fearing the danger of this cruel mirage, he went down the opposite side of the hill to that by which he had come up the day before.

The remains of a rug showed that this place of refuge had at one time been inhabited; at a short distance he saw some palm trees full of dates. Then the instinct which binds us to life awoke again in his heart. He hoped to live long enough to await the passing of some Arabs, or perhaps he might hear the sound of cannon; for at this time Bonaparte was traversing Egypt.

This thought gave him new life. The palm tree seemed to bend with the weight of the ripe fruit. He shook some of it down. When he tasted this unhoped-for manna, he felt sure that the palms had been cultivated by a former inhabitant—the savory, fresh meat of the dates was proof of the care of his predecessor. He passed suddenly from dark despair to an almost insane joy. He went up again to the top of the hill, and spent the rest of the day in cutting down one of sterile palm trees, which the night before had served him for shelter. A vague memory made him think of the animals of the desert; and in case they might come to drink at the spring, visible from the base of the rocks but lost farther down, he resolved to guard himself from their visits by placing a barrier at the entrance of his hermitage.

In spite of his diligence, and the strength which the fear of being devoured asleep gave him, he was unable to cut the palm in pieces, though he succeeded in cutting it down. At eventide the king of the desert fell; the sound of its fall resounded far and wide, like a sigh in the solitude; the soldier shuddered as though he had heard some voice predicting woe.

But like an heir who does not long bewail a deceased parent, he tore off from this beautiful tree the tall broad green leaves which are its poetic adornment, and used them to mend the mat on which he was to sleep.

Fatigued by the heat and his work, he fell asleep under the red curtains of his wet cave.

In tne middle of the night his sleep was troubled by an extraordinary noise; he sat up, and the deep silence around him allowed him to distinguish the alternative accents of a respiration whose savage energy could not belong to a human creature.

A profound terror, increased still further by the darkness, the silence, and his waking images, froze his heart within him. He almost felt his hair stand on end, when by straining his eyes to their utmost he perceived through the shadows two faint yellow lights. At first he attributed these lights to the reflection of his own pupils, but soon the vivid brilliance of the night aided him gradually to distinguish the objects around him in the cave, and he beheld a huge animal lying but two steps from him. Was it a lion, a tiger, or a crocodile?

The Provençal was not educated enough to know under what species his enemy ought to be classed; but his fright was all the greater, as his ignorance led him to imagine all terrors at once; he endured a cruel torture, noting every variation of the breathing close to him without daring to make the slightest movement. An odor, pungent like that of a fox, but more penetrating, profounder—so to speak—filled the cave, and when the Provençal became sensible of this, his terror reached its height, for he could not longer doubt the proximity of a terrible companion, whose royal dwelling served him for shelter.

Presently the reflection of the moon, descending on the horizon, lit up the den, rendering gradually visible and resplendent the spotted skin of a panther. .

This lion of Egypt slept, curled up like a big dog, the peaceful possessor of a sumptuous niche at the gate of an *hôtel;* its eyes opened for a moment and closed again; its face was turned toward the man. A thousand confused thoughts passed through the Frenchman's mind; first he thought of killing it with a bullet from his gun, but he saw there was not enough distance between them for him to take proper aim—the shot would miss the mark. And if it were to wake!—the thought made his limbs rigid. He listened to his own heart beating in the midst of the silence, and cursed the too violent pulsations which the flow of blood brought on, fearing to disturb that sleep which allowed him time to think of some means of escape.

Twice he placed his hand on his scimitar, intending to cut off the head of his enemy; but the difficulty of cutting the stiff, short hair compelled him to abandon this daring project. To miss would be to die for certain, he thought; he preferred the chances of fair fight, and made up his mind to wait till morning; the morning did not leave him long to wait.

He could now examine the panther at ease; its muzzle was smeared with blood.

"She's had a good dinner," he thought, without troubling himself as to whether her feast might have been on human flesh. "She won't be hungry when she gets up."

It was a female. The fur on her belly and flanks was glistening white; many small marks like velvet formed beautiful bracelets round her feet; her sinuous tail was also white, ending with black rings; the overpart of her dress, yellow like unburnished gold, very lissom and soft, had the characteristic blotches in the form of rosettes, which distinguish the panther from every other feline species.

This tranquil and formidable hostess snored in an attitude as graceful as that of a cat lying on a cushion.

Ier blood-stained paws, nervous and well-armed, were tretched out before her face, which rested upon them, ind from which radiated her straight, slender whisk-rs, like threads of silver.

If she had been like that in a cage, the Provençal vould doubtless have admired the grace of the animal, ind the vigorous contrasts of vivid color which gave ner robe an imperial splendor; but just then his sight vas troubled by her sinister appearance.

The presence of the panther, even asleep, could not fail to produce the effect which the magnetic eyes of the serpent are said to have on the nightingale.

For a moment the courage of the soldier began to fail before this danger, though no doubt it would have risen at the mouth of a cannon charged with shell. Nevertheless, a bold thought brought daylight to his soul and sealed up the source of the cold sweat which sprang forth on his brow. Like men driven to bay who defy death and offer their body to the smiter, so he, seeing in this merely a tragic episode, resolved to play his part with honor to the last.

"The day before yesterday the Arabs would have killed me perhaps," he said; so considering himself as good as dead already, he waited bravely, with excited curiosity, his enemy's awakening.

When the sun appeared, the panther suddenly opened her eyes; then she put out her paws with energy, as if to stretch them and get rid of cramp. At last she yawned, showing the formidable apparatus of her teeth and pointed tongue, rough as a file.

"A regular *petite maitresse*," thought the Frenchman, seeing her roll herself about so softly and coquettishly. She licked off the blood which stained her

paws and muzzle, and scratched her head with reiter-
ated gestures full of prettiness. "All right, make a little
toilet," the Frenchman said to himself, beginning to
recover his gaiety with his courage; "we'll say good
morning to each other presently," and he seized the
small, short dagger which he had taken from the Mangrabins. At this moment the panther turned her
head toward the man and looked at him fixedly without moving.

The rigidity of her metallic eyes and their insupportable luster made him shudder, especially when the
animal walked toward him. But he looked at her
caressingly, staring into her eyes in order to magnetize
her, and let her come quite close to him; then with a
movement both gentle and amorous, as though he were
caressing the most beautiful of women, he passed his
hand over her whole body, from the head to the tail,
scratching the flexible vertebræ which divided the panther's yellow back. The animal waved her tail volup-
tuously, and her eyes grew gentle; and when for the
third time the Frenchman accomplished this interesting
flattery, she gave forth one of those purrings by which
our cats express their pleasure; but this murmur issued from a throat so powerful and so deep, that it
resounded through the cave like the last vibrations of
an organ in a church. The man, understanding the
importance of his caresses, redoubled them in such a
way as to surprise and stupefy his imperious courtesan.
When he felt sure of having extinguished the ferocity
of his capricious companion, whose hunger had so fortunately been satisfied the day before, he got up to go
out of the cave; the panther let him go out, but when
he had reached the summit of the hill she sprang with

the lightness of a sparrow hopping from twig to twig, and rubbed herself against his legs, putting up her back after the manner of all the race of cats. Then regarding her guest with eyes whose glare had softened a little, she gave vent to that wild cry which naturalists compare to the grating of a saw.

"She is exacting," said the Frenchman, smiling.

He was bold enough to play with her ears; he caressed her belly and scratched her head as hard as he could.

When he saw that he was successful, he tickled her skull with the point of his dagger, watching for the right moment to kill her, but the hardness of her bones made him tremble for his success.

The sultana of the desert showed herself gracious to her slave; she lifted her head, stretched out her neck, and manifested her delight by the tranquillity of her attitude. It suddenly occurred to the soldier that to kill this savage princess with one blow he must poignard her in the throat.

He raised the blade, when the panther, satisfied no doubt, laid herself gracefully at his feet, and cast up at him glances in which, in spite of their natural fierceness, was mingled confusedly a kind of good-will. The poor Provençal ate his dates, leaning against one of the palm trees, and casting his eyes alternately on the desert in quest of some liberator and on his terrible companion to watch her uncertain clemency.

The panther looked at the place where the date stones fell, and every time that he threw one down her eyes expressed an incredible mistrust.

She examined the man with an almost commercial prudence. However, this examination was favorable

to him, for when he had finished his meager meal she
licked his boots with her powerful rough tongue,
brushing off with marvellous skill the dust gathered in
the creases.

"Ah, but when she's really hungry!" thought the
Frenchman. In spite of the shudder this thought
caused him, the soldier began to measure curiously the
proportions of the panther, certainly one of the most
splendid specimens of its race. She was three feet
high and four feet long without counting her tail; this
powerful weapon, rounded like a cudgel, was nearly
three feet long. The head, large as that of a lioness,
was distinguished by a rare expression of refinement.
The cold cruelty of a tiger was dominant, it was true,
but there was also a vague resemblance to the face of
a sensual woman. Indeed, the face of this solitary
queen had something of the gaiety of a drunken Nero;
she had satiated herself with blood, and she wanted to
play.

The soldier tried if he might walk up and down, and
the panther left him free, contenting herself with following him with her eyes, less like a faithful dog than
a big Angora cat, observing everything, and every
movement of her master.

When he looked round, he saw, by the spring, the
remains of his horse; the panther had dragged the
carcass all that way; about two-thirds of it had been
devoured already. The sight reassured him.

It was easy to explain the panther's absence, and
the respect she had had for him while he slept. The
first piece of good luck emboldened him to tempt the
future, and he conceived the wild hope of continuing
on good terms with the panther during the entire day,

neglecting no means of taming her and remaining in her good graces.

He returned to her, and had the unspeakable joy of seeing her wag her tail with an almost imperceptible movement at his approach. He sat down then, without fear, by her side, and they began to play together; he took her paws and muzzle, pulled her ears, rolled her over on her back, stroked her warm, delicate flanks. She let him do whatever he liked, and when he began to stroke the hair on her feet she drew her claws in carefully.

The man, keeping the dagger in one hand, thought to plunge it into the belly of the too-confiding panther, but he was afraid that he would be immediately strangled in her last convulsive struggle; besides, he felt in his heart a sort of remorse which bid him respect a creature that had done him no harm. He seemed to have found a friend, in a boundless desert; half unconsciously he thought of his first sweetheart, whom he had nicknamed "Mignonne" by way of contrast, because she was so atrociously jealous that all the time of their love he was in fear of the knife with which she had always threatened him.

This memory of his early days suggested to him the idea of making the young panther answer to this name, now that he began to admire with less terror her swiftness, suppleness, and softness. Toward the end of the day he had familiarized himself with his perilous position; he now almost liked the painfulness of it. At last his companion had got into the habit of looking up at him whenever he cried in a falsetto voice, "Mignonne."

At the setting of the sun Mignonne gave, several

times running, a profound melancholy cry. "She's
been well brought up," said the light-hearted soldier;
"she says her prayers." But this mental joke only occurred to him when he noticed what a pacific attitude
his companion remained in. "Come, *ma petite blonde,*
I'll let you go to bed first," he said to her, counting
on the activity of his own legs to run away as quickly
as possible, directly she was asleep, and seek another
shelter for the night.

The soldier waited with impatience the hour of his
flight, and when it had arrived he walked vigorously in
the direction of the Nile; but hardly had he made a
quarter of a league in the sand when he heard the panther bounding after him, crying with that saw-like cry
more dreadful even than the sound of her leaping.

"Ah!" he said, "then she's taken a fancy to me; she
has never met any one before, and it is really quite
flattering to have her first love." That instant the man
fell into one of those movable quicksands so terrible to
travellers and from which it is impossible to save oneself. Feeling himself caught, he gave a shriek of
alarm; the panther seized him with her teeth by the
collar, and, springing vigorously backward, drew him
as if by magic out of the whirling sand.

"Ah, Mignonne!" cried the soldier, caressing her
enthusiastically; "we're bound together for life and
death—but no jokes, mind!" and he retraced his steps.

From that time the desert seemed inhabited. It
contained a being to whom the man could talk, and
whose ferocity was rendered gentle by him, though
he could not explain to himself the reason for their
strange friendship. Great as was the soldier's desire
to stay upon guard, he slept.

On awakening he could not find Mignonne; he
mounted the hill, and in the distance saw her springing
toward him after the habit of these animals, who cannot run on account of the extreme flexibility of the
vertebral column. Mignonne arrived, her jaws covered
with blood; she received the wonted caress of her companion, showing with much purring how happy it made
her. Her eyes, full of languor, turned still more gently
than the day before toward the Provençal, who talked
to her as one would to a tame animal.

"Ah! Mademoiselle, you are a nice girl, aren't you?
Just look at that! so we like to be made much of, don't
we? Aren't you ashamed of yourself? So you have
been eating some Arab or other, have you? that doesn't
matter. They're animals just the same as you are; but
don't you take to eating Frenchmen, or I shan't like
you any longer."

She played like a dog with its master, letting herself
be rolled over, knocked about, and stroked, alternately;
sometimes she herself would provoke the soldier, putting up her paw with a soliciting gesture.

Some days passed in this manner. The companion-
ship permitted the Provençal to appreciate the sublime beauty of the desert; now that he had a living
thing to think about, alternations of fear and quiet,
and plenty to eat, his mind became filled with contrast
and his life began to be diversified.

Solitude revealed to him all her secrets, and enveloped him in her delights. He discovered in the rising
and setting of the sun sights unknown to the world.
He knew what it was to tremble when he heard over
his head the hiss of a bird's wing, so rarely did they
pass, or when he saw the clouds, changing and many-

colored travellers, melt one into another. He studied
in the night time the effect of the moon upon the ocean
of sand, where the simoon made waves swift of movement and rapid in their change. He lived the life of
the Eastern day, marvelling at its wonderful pomp;
then, after having revelled in the sight of a hurricane
over the plain where the whirling sands made red, dry
mists and death-bearing clouds, he would welcome the
night with joy, for then fell the healthful freshness of
the stars, and he listened to imaginary music in the
skies. Then solitude taught him to unroll the treasures
of dreams. He passed whole hours in remembering
mere nothings, and comparing his present life with his
past.

At last he grew passionately fond of the panther;
for some sort of affection was a necessity.

Whether it was that his will powerfully projected
had modified the character of his companion, or
whether, because she found abundant food in her
predatory excursions in the deserts, she respected the
man's life, he began to fear for it no longer, seeing her
so well tamed.

He devoted the greater part of his time to sleep, but
he was obliged to watch like a spider in its web that
the moment of his deliverance might not escape him,
if any one should pass the line marked by the horizon.
He had sacrificed his shirt to make a flag with, which
he hung at the top of a palm tree, whose foliage he had
torn off. Taught by necessity, he found the means of
keeping it spread out, by fastening it with little sticks;
for the wind might not be blowing at the moment when
the passing traveller was looking through the desert.

It was during the long hours, when he had abandoned hope, that he amused himself with the panther. He had come to learn the different inflections of her voice, the expressions of her eyes; he had studied the capricious patterns of all the rosettes which marked the gold of her robe. Mignonne was not even angry when he took hold of the tuft at the end of her tail to count the rings, those graceful ornaments which glittered in the sun like jewelry. It gave him pleasure to contemplate the supple, fine outlines of her form, the whiteness of her belly, the graceful pose of her head. But it was especially when she was playing that he felt most pleasure in looking at her; the agility and youthful lightness of her movements were a continual surprise to him; he wondered at the supple way in which she jumped and climbed, washed herself and arranged her fur, crouched down and prepared to spring. However rapid her spring might be, however slippery the stone she was on, she would always stop short at the word "Mignonne."

One day, in a bright mid-day sun, an enormous bird coursed through the air. The man left his panther to look at this new guest; but after waiting a moment the deserted sultana growled deeply.

"My goodness! I do believe she's jealous," he cried, seeing her eyes become hard again; "the soul of Virginie has passed into her body; that's certain."

The eagle disappeared into the air, while the soldier admired the curved contour of the panther.

But there was such youth and grace in her form! she was beautiful as a woman! the blond fur of her robe mingled well with the delicate tints of faint white which marked her flanks.

The profuse light cast down by the sun made this

living gold, these russet markings, to burn in a way to give them an indefinable attraction.

The man and the panther looked at one another with a look full of meaning; the coquette quivered when she felt her friend stroke her head; her eyes flashed like lightning—then she shut them tightly.

"She has a soul," he said, looking at the stillness of this queen of the sands, golden like them, white like them, solitary and burning like them.

.   .   .   .   .

"Well," she said, "I have read your plea in favor of beasts; but how did two so well adapted to understand each other end?"

"Ah, well! you see, they ended as all great passions do end—by a misunderstanding. For some reason one suspects the other of treason; they don't come to an explanation through pride, and quarrel and part from sheer obstinacy."

"Yet sometimes at the best moments a single word or a look is enough—but anyhow go on with your story."

"It's horribly difficult, but you will understand, after what the old villain told me over his champagne.

"He said—'I don't know if I hurt her, but she turned round, as if enraged, and with her sharp teeth caught hold of my leg—gently, I daresay; but I, thinking she would devour me, plunged my dagger into her throat. She rolled over, giving a cry that froze my heart; and I saw her dying, still looking at me without anger. I would have given all the world —my cross even, which I had not got then—to have brought her to life again. It was as though I had murdered a real person; and the soldiers who had seen my flag, and were come to my assistance, found me in tears.'

" 'Well, sir,' he said, after a moment of silence, 'since then I have been in war in Germany, in Spain, in Russia, in France; I've certainly carried my carcass about a good deal, but never have I seen anything like the desert. Ah! yes, it is very beautiful!'

" 'What did you feel there?' I asked him.

" 'Oh! that can't be described, young man. Besides, I am not always regretting my palm trees and my panther. I should have to be very melancholy for that. In the desert, you see, there is everything, and nothing.'

" 'Yes, but explain——'

" 'Well,' he said, with an impatient gesture, 'it is God without mankind.' "

LOST BY A LAUGH

LOST BY A LAUGH

"DURING the campaign of 1812," said General Montriveau, "I was the involuntary cause of a terrible calamity. You, Doctor Bianchon, who study the mind so carefully when you study the human body, may perhaps find in this story a solution to some of your problems on the Will.

"It was my second campaign. Like the simple young lieutenant of artillery, I loved danger and laughed at everything.

"When we reached the Beresina, the army—as you know—was utterly disorganized and without any idea of military discipline. In fact, it was a mere crowd of men of all nations moving instinctively from north to south. The soldiers would drive away a ragged, bare-footed general from their camp-fires if he did not bring them food or fuel. Even after the passing of this celebrated river the confusion was as great as before.

"I had come quitely through the marshes of Zembin all alone, and was walking on, searching for a house where some one would take me in. Not finding one, or being driven away from those which I did find, toward evening I was fortunate enough to light upon a wretched little Polish farm. Nothing could give you an idea of the place unless you have seen the wooden houses of Lower Normandy or the poorest *métairies* of La Beauce. These dwellings consist of one single room divided off at one end by a partition of boards, the smaller portion serving as a place to store fodder in. Although the twilight was growing dim, I had descried in the distance a thin line of smoke arising from this house. Hoping to find companions more compassionate than those to whom I had as yet addressed myself, I marched on bravely to the farm. I went in and found several officers seated at table, eating horse-flesh broiled over the coals, frozen beet-root, and potatoes. With them—no unusual sight —was a woman. I recognized two or three of the men as artillery captains belonging to the first regiment in which I had served. They greeted me with hurrahs and acclamations that would have surprised me indeed on the other side of the Beresina; but just then the cold was less intense, my comrades were enjoying rest and warmth and food, the floor strewn with trusses of straw, and altogether there seemed to be a prospect of passing a comfortable night. After all it was not much that we asked for then. My brother officers were philanthropists, when they could be so for nothing;—by the way, one of the most usual modes of philanthropy. I sat down upon a heap of fodder and fell to.

"At the end of the table, on the side of the door communicating with the little room full of hay and straw, sat my former colonel. Among all the motley crowd of men whom it has been my lot to meet, he was one of the most extraordinary. He was an Italian. In southern countries, whenever human nature is fine, it is sublime. I do not know whether you have noticed the wonderful whiteness of Italians when their com-

plexion is fair—it is marvellous—in the sunlight
especially. When I read the fanciful portrait of Colonel Oudet which Charles Nodier has drawn us, I
found my own impressions in every one of his polished
sentences. An Italian, like the majority of the officers of
his regiment—otherwise drafted by the Emperor from
the *armée d'Eugène*—my colonel was a man of lofty
stature, eight or nine *pouces* high, admirably proportioned, a trifle stout perhaps, but of enormous strength,
and as agile and wiry as a gray-hound. In contrast
with a profusion of black curls, the whiteness of the
skin gleamed like a woman's. He had small hands,
beautiful feet, and a gracious mouth; his nose was
aquiline and finely formed, naturally pinched in at the
point; in his frequent outbursts of passion it grew
perfectly pallid.

"Indeed the violence of his temper was so incredible,
words would fail to describe it; but the sequel affords
abundant proof. No one could remain unmoved before it. Perhaps I myself was the only person who
was not afraid of him; but then he had conceived an
extraordinary friendship for me. Whatever I did was
right. When this passion was upon him, the muscles
of his brow contracted, and formed a Delta, or rather
the horse-shoe of *Redgauntlet,* in the middle of his
forehead. This mark struck you perhaps with even
more terror than the magnetic sparks which flashed
from his blue eyes. Then his whole body quivered,
and his strength, ordinarily enormous, became almost
boundless. He spoke with a strong *grasseyement,* and
his voice, at least as powerful as the voice of the Oudet
of Charles Nodier, threw an incredible richness of
tone into the consonant or syllable on which the *grass-*

eyement fell. If at certain moments this Parisian vulgarism of pronunciation was an additional charm in him, you must actually have heard it to conceive what a sense of power it conveyed when he gave the word of command or spoke under the influence of emotion. When he was calm his blue eyes beamed with angelic sweetness, and his clear-cut brow bore an expression full of charm. At a parade of the *armée d'Italie* there was not a man who could compare with him; and at the time of the last review which Napoleon held before we crossed the Russian frontier, even d'Orsay himself—the handsome d'Orsay—was surpassed by our colonel. This favored being was a mass of contradictions. Contrast is the essence of Passion. You need not ask me then whether he exercised over women that irresistible influence before which our nature yields like liquid glass beneath the blower's pipe. However, by a strange fatality which perhaps a keen observer might explain, the colonel failed or refused to make more than a very few conquests.

"To give you an idea of his violence, I will tell you in a few words what I saw him do in one of these paroxysms of rage. One day we were ascending with our cannon a very narrow road that had a deep cutting on one side and a wood on the other. In the middle of the ascent we met another regiment of artillery headed by its colonel. This colonel tried to make the captain in command of the first battery of our regiment give way. Naturally enough the captain refused; so their colonel made a sign to his own first battery to advance. Notwithstanding the care which the driver took to keep as close to the wood as possible, the wheel of the first gun-carriage caught our captain's

right leg and broke the bone clean in two, hurling him
off his horse on the opposite side. It was all done in a
moment. Our colonel, who was only a little way off,
guessing what the whole quarrel was about, gallops up
at full speed, right through the wood and our artillery
—we thought every instant his horse must have gone
down, head over heels—and arrives on the scene in
front of the other colonel, just at the moment that our
captain cried out 'Help,' and fell. Well, our Italian
colonel was no longer a human being! Foam burst
from his mouth like the froth of champagne—he
growled like a lion. Incapable of articulating a syllable,
or even a cry, he made a terrible sign to his oppo-
nent, pointed to the wood, and drew his sword. The
two colonels entered the wood. In a couple of seconds
we saw the aggressor stretched on the ground, his
head cleft in two by our colonel's sword. The men of
the other regiment fell back;—the Deuce! and pretty
quick too. Our captain—who was almost killed, and
lay moaning in the mud where the wheel of the gun-
carriage had thrown him—had a wife, a most charming Italian, from Messina. She was not altogether indifferent to our colonel. It was this circumstance
which had added fuel to his fury. Her husband was
entitled to his protection; it was his duty to defend the
man as much as the woman herself.

"Now in the cabin beyond Zembin, where I had received such a warm welcome, this very captain sat opposite me, and his wife was at the other side of the
table, opposite the colonel. She was a little woman,
this Messinian, and very dark; her eyes were black and
almond-shaped, within them glowed all the fervor of
the Sicilian sun; her name was Rosina. Just at that

time she was pitiably thin; her cheeks, like fruit exposed to all the rough chances of the wayside, were
stained with dust. Though she was worn out with
travelling, scarcely covered by her rags, her hair
matted and in disorder, muffled in the fragment of a
shawl, yet there was still somewhat of the charm of
womanhood about her. Her graceful gestures, her
curled red lips, her white teeth, the outline of her face,
the form of her breasts, these were charms which cold
and want and misery could not quite efface; to men who
still could think of women, they still spoke of love.
Besides, Rosina possessed one of those natures apparently frail, but in reality full of nerve and power.

"The face of her husband, a Piedmontese, suggested (if one can combine two such ideas) a sort of
mocking good-nature. He was a gentleman, brave,
and well educated, but he appeared to ignore the relations which had been existing for nearly three years
between his wife and the colonel. I used to attribute
this indifference to Italian manners, or to some home
secret of their own. Still there was something in the
man's face which always inspired me with an involuntary distrust. His lower lip was thin and very flexible, and turned down at the corners instead of up; this
feature seemed to me to betray an undercurrent of
cruelty in a character apparently indolent and phleg-
matic.

"You may easily imagine that the conversation when
I arrived was not of a very brilliant order. My comrades were worn out, and ate in silence. Of course
they asked me a few questions, and we told each other
our troubles, interspersing our stories with remarks on
the campaign, the cold, the generals and their mistakes,

and the Russians. A moment or two after my arrival, the colonel, having finished his meager repast, wipes his mustache, wishes us good night, looks with his dark eyes at the Italian, and says to her: 'Rosina.' Then without waiting for an answer, he goes to pass the night in the little store-room where the fodder was kept.

"It was not difficult to guess the meaning of the colonel's summons. Besides, the young woman allowed an indescribable gesture to escape her, which expressed not only the displeasure she must have felt at seeing their connection thus proclaimed abroad without any respect of persons, but also her consciousness of the insult offered both to her own dignity as a woman and to her husband. But more still the twitching of all her features, and the violent contraction of her eyebrows, seemed to betray a sort of presentiment; perhaps she had some instinct of her fate. She sat on quietly at the table. A moment afterward, probably as the colonel lay down in his hay or straw bed, he repeated 'Rosina.' The accent of this second appeal was still more brutally interrogative than the first. All the impatience, the despotism, the will of the man were expressed in that *grasseyement* of his, and his Italian elongation of the vowels and consonants in those three syllables. Rosina grew pale, but she rose, passed out behind us and went to the colonel.

"All my comrades preserved a profound silence; but I unhappily, after looking at them all round, began to laugh, and then my laughter was repeated from mouth to mouth.

" '*Tu ridi,*' said the husband.

" '*Ma foi! mon camarade!*' said I, becoming serious

again, 'I acknowledge that I am in the wrong; I am sure I beg your pardon most heartily, and if you are not content with my apologies I am ready to give you satisfaction.'

" 'It is not you who are in the wrong, but I,' he replied coldly.

"After this we lay down for the night in the room where we were, and soon were all sound asleep.

"The next day, each man, without waking his neighbor or seeking a companion for the journey, started off again as his fancy led him. It was this sort of egoism which made our retreat one of the most terrible dramas of selfishness, misery, and horror, ever played out under Heaven.

"However, about seven or eight hundred paces from our lodging, we all met again—almost all—and marched on together, one same necessity impelling us. We were like geese driven in flocks by the blind despotism of a child. When we had reached a mound, from whence the farm where we had spent the night was still in view, we heard cries like the bellowing of bulls, or the roaring of lions in the desert; but no—it was a din that cannot be compared to any sound known to man. However, mingled with this ominous, horrible roaring, we could distinguish the feeble cries of a woman. We all turned round, a prey to an indescribable feeling of terror. The house was no longer visible; it had been barricaded, and was nothing but a pile of flame. Volumes of smoke, carried away by the wind, bore toward us these hoarse and hideous sounds, and with them a strong, unspeakable odor.

"A few paces from us came the captain, walking up quickly to join our caravan. We all looked at him in silence, no one dared to question him; but he, divining our curiosity, pointed with his right hand to his own breast and with his left to the fire, and said, '*Son' io!*'

"We continued our march without making a single remark."

.   .   .   .   .

"There is nothing more horrible than the rebellion of a sheep," said de Marsay.

GOLD

GOLD

At this time I was living in a little street which no doubt you do not know, la rue de Lesdiguières; it begins in la rue Saint Antoine, opposite a fountain near la place de la Bastille, and ends in la rue de la Cerisaie. The love of science had thrown me into a garret where I worked all through the night; the day I spent at a neighboring library, le Bibliothèque de Monsieur. I lived frugally, accepting all the conditions of monastic life—conditions so necessary to men at work. When the weather was fine, the farthest I went was for a walk on le boulevard Bourdon. One passion alone drew me out of my studious habits; but even that was a study in itself. I used to go and watch the manners of the *faubourg*, its inhabitants and their characters. As I was as ill-clad as the workmen and indifferent to appearances, I did not in any way put them on their guard against me; I was able to mix with them when they stood in groups, and watch them driving their bargains and disputing as they were leaving their work. With me observation had even then become intuitive; it did not neglect the body, but it penetrated further, into the soul, or rather, it grasped the exterior details so perfectly, that it at once passed beyond. It gave me the faculty of living the life of the individual upon whom it exercised itself, by allowing me to sub-

153

stitute myself for him, like the dervish in the Thous-and-and-One-Nights, who took possession of the body and soul of people over whom he pronounced certain words.

Between eleven and twelve o'clock at night I might fall in with a workman and his wife returning to-gether from the Ambigu Comique; then I would amuse myself by following them from le boulevard du Pon-taux-Choux to le boulevard Beaumarchais. First of all, the good people would talk about the piece they had seen; then, from the thread to the needle, they passed on to their own affairs. The mother would drag along her child by the hand without listening to his cries or his questions. Then the pair would count up the money to be paid them next day, and spend it in twenty different ways. Then there were details in housekeeping, grumblings about the enormous price of potatoes, or the length of the winter and the dear-ness of fuel; and then forcible representations as to what was owing to the baker; at last the discussion grew acrimonious, and each of them would betray his character in forcible expressions. As I listened to these people I was able to enter into their life; I felt their rags upon my back, and walked with my feet in their worn-out shoes; their desires, their wants—everything passed into my soul, or else it was my soul that passed into theirs. It was the dream of a man awake. I grew warm with them against some tyranni-cal foreman, or the bad customers who made them re-turn many times without paying them. To be quit of one's own habits, to become another than oneself by an inebriation of the moral faculties, and to play this game at will—this formed my distraction.

To what do I owe this gift? Is it a kind of second sight? Is it one of those qualities which, if abused, induce madness? I have never sought to find the cause of this power; I possess it and I use it, that is all. It is enough to know that, at that time, I had decomposed the elements of the heterogeneous mass called the People—that I had analyzed it in such a way that I could set their proper value on its qualities, good and bad. I knew already the possible usefulness of the *faubourg*, that seminary of Revolution which contains heroes, inventors, men of practical science, rogues, villains, virtues and vices, all oppressed by misery, stifled by poverty, drowned in wine, worn out by strong drink. You could not imagine how many unknown adventures, how many forgotten dramas, how many horrible and beautiful things lie hidden in this town of sorrow. Imagination will never reach the truth that lurks there, for no man can go to seek it out, the descent is too deep to discover its marvellous scenes of tragedy and comedy, its masterpieces which are born of chance.

I know not why I have kept the story I am about to relate so long without telling it; it is part of those strange tales stored in the bag whence memory draws them capriciously, like the numbers of a lottery. I have many more of them, as strange as this and as deeply buried; they will have their turn, I assure you.

One day my housekeeper, the wife of a workman, came to ask me to honor with my presence the marriage of one of her sisters. To make you understand what this marriage must have been like, I must tell you that I gave the poor creature forty *sous* a month; for this she came every morning to make my bed,

clean my shoes, brush my clothes, sweep the room, and
get ready my *déjeûner;* the rest of her time she went
to turn the handle of a machine, earning at this hard
work ten *sous* a day. Her husband, a cabinet-maker,
earned four *francs.* But as they had a family of three
children, it was almost impossible for them to get an
honest living. I never met with more thorough honesty than this man's and woman's. For five years
after my leaving the district, *la mère Vaillant* used to
come to congratulate me on my name day, and bring
me a bouquet and some oranges,—and she was a
woman who could never manage to save ten *sous.*
Misery had drawn us together. I have never been able
to give her more than ten *francs,* often borrowed on
purpose. This may explain my promise to go to the
wedding; I relied upon effacing myself in the poor
creature's merriment.

The marriage feast, the ball, the whole entertain-
ment took place on the first floor of a wine shop in
la rue de Charenton. The room was large, papered up
to the height of the tables with a filthy paper, and lit
by lamps with tin reflectors; along the walls were
wooden benches; in this room were twenty-four people,
all dressed in their best, decked with large bouquets
and ribands, their faces flushed, full of the excitement
of the *courtille,* dancing as if the world were coming to
an end. The bride and bridegroom were embracing
to the general satisfaction, and certain hee-hees! and
haw-haws! were heard, facetious, but really less in-
decent than the timid glances of girls who have been well
brought up. The whole company expressed an animal
contentment, which was somehow or other contagious.
However, neither the physiognomies of the company,

nor the wedding, nor in fact any of these people, have any connection with my story. Only bear in mind the strangeness of the frame. Picture to yourself the squalid, red shop, sniff the odor of the wine, listen to the howls of merriment, linger a while in this *faubourg,* among those workmen and poor women and old men who had given themselves up to pleasure for a single night!

The orchestra was composed of three blind men from Les Quinze-Vingts; the first was violin, the second clarionet, and the third flageolet. They were paid seven *francs* for the night among the three. You may imagine they did not give Rossini or Beethoven at that price; they played what they chose or could; with charming delicacy, no one reproached them. Their music did such brutal violence to the drum of my ear, that, after glancing round at the company, I looked at the blind trio,—I was inclined to indulgence at once, when I recognized their uniform. The performers were in the embrasure of a window, so that you were obliged to be close to them to be able to distinguish their features; I did not go up immediately, but when I did get near them, I do not know how it was, but it was all over, the wedding party and the music disappeared; my curiosity was excited to the highest degree, for my soul passed into the body of the man who played the clarionet. The violin and the flageolet had both quite ordinary faces, the usual face of the blind, intense, attentive, and grave; but the clarionet's was a phenomenon such as arrests and absorbs the attention of a philosopher or an artist.

Imagine a plaster mask of Dante, lit up by the red glow of the *quinquet* lamp and crowned with a forest of silver-white hair. The bitter, sorrowful expression of this magnificent head was intensified by blindness, for thought gave a new life to the dead eyes; it was as if a scorching light came forth from them, the product of one single, incessant desire, itself inscribed in vigorous lines upon a prominent brow, scored with wrinkles, like the courses of stone in an old wall. The old man breathed into his instrument at random, without paying the least attention to the measure of the air; his fingers rose and fell as they moved the worn-out keys with mechanical unconsciousness; he did not trouble himself about making what are called in orchestral terms *canards,* but the dancers did not notice it any more than did my Italian's two acolytes; for I was determined he must be an Italian, and he was an Italian. There was something great and despotic in this old Homer keeping within himself an Odyssey doomed to oblivion. It was such real greatness that it still triumphed over its abject condition, a despotism so full of life that it dominated his poverty.

None of the violent passions which lead a man to good as well as to evil, and make of him a convict or a hero, were wanting in that grandly hewn, lividly Italian face. The whole was overshadowed by grizzled eyebrows which cast into shade the deep hollows beneath; one trembled lest one should see the light of thought reappear in them, as one fears to see brigands armed with torches and daggers come to the mouth of a cave. A lion dwelt within that cage of flesh, a lion whose rage was exhausted in vain against the iron of its bar. The flame of despair had sunk quenched into its ashes, the lava had grown cold; but its channels, its destructions, a little smoke, bore evidence to the violence of the eruption and the ravages of the fire. These ideas revealed in the man's appearance were as burning in his soul as they were cold upon his face.

Between dances the violin and the flageolet, gravely occupied with their bottle and glass, hung their instruments on to the bottom of their reddish-colored coats, stretched out their hand toward a little table placed in the embrasure of the window and on which was their canteen, and offered a full glass to the Italian; —he could not take it himself, as the table was always behind his chair;—he thanked them by a friendly gesture of the head. Their movements were accomplished with that precision which is always so astonishing in the blind of Les Quinze-Vingts, it almost makes you believe that they can see.

Presently I went up nearer to the three blind men, so as to be better able to listen to them; but when I was close to them they began to study me, and not, I suppose, recognizing a workman, they remained shy.

"What country do you come from, you who are playing the clarionet?"

"From Venice," replied the blind man, with a slight Italian accent.

"Were you born blind, or did you become blind from——?"

"From an accident," he replied sharply; "it was a cursed cataract."

"Venice is a fine town; I have always had a longing to go there."

The old man's face lit up, his wrinkles worked, he was deeply moved.

"If I went there with you," he said, "you would not be losing your time."

"Don't talk to him about Venice," said the violin, "or you'll start our Doge off; especially as he has already put two bottles into his mouthpiece—has our prince!"

"Come, let's go on, *père Canard,*" said the flageolet.

They all three began to play; but all the time they took to execute four country dances, the Venetian kept sniffing after me, he divined the excessive curiosity which I felt about him. His expression lost the cold, sad look; some hope—I know not what—enlivened all his features and ran like a blue flame through his wrinkles; he smiled and wiped his bold, terrible brow; in fact he grew cheerful, like a man getting on to his hobby.

"How old are you?" I asked.

"Eighty-two!"

"How long have you been blind?"

"Nearly fifty years," he replied, with an accent which showed that his regrets did not arise only from his loss of sight, but from some great power of which he must have been despoiled.

"Why is it they call you the Doge?" I asked.

"Oh, it's their joke," he said. "I am a patrician of Venice, and might have been Doge like the rest."

"What is your name then?"

"Here, le père Canet," he said. "My name could never be written on the registers different from that; but in Italian it is Marco Facino Cane, principe di Varese."

"Why! you are descended from the famous *condottiere* Facino Cane, whose conquests passed to the Duke of Milan?"

"*E vero,*" said he. "In those days the son of Cane

took refuge in Venice to avoid being killed by the Visconti, and got himself inscribed in the Golden Book. But now there is no Cane, any more than there is a book." And he made a terrible gesture of extinct patriotism and disgust for human affairs.

"But if you were a Senator of Venice, you must have been rich; how did you come to lose your fortune?"

At this question he raised his head toward me with a truly tragic movement as if to examine me, and answered, "By misfortune!"

He no longer thought of drinking, and refused by a sign the glass of wine which the old flageolet was just at that moment holding out to him, then his head sank. These details were not of a kind to extinguish my curiosity. While these three machines were playing a country dance, I watched the old Venetian noble with the feelings which devour a man of twenty. I saw Venice and the Adriatic; I saw her in ruins in the ruins of his face. I walked in that city that is so dear to its inhabitants. I went from the Rialto to the Grand Canal, from the Quay of the Slaves to the Lido; I came back to the unique, sublime Cathedral; I examined the casements of the Casa d'Oro, each with its different ornament; I gazed at the ancient palaces with all their wealth of marble; in a word, I saw all those marvels with which the *savant* sympathizes the more because he can color them to his liking, and does not rob his dreams of their poetry by the sight of the reality. I followed back the course of the life of this scion of the greatest of the *condottieri*, and sought to discover in him the traces of his misfortunes, and the causes of the physical and moral degradation which rendered yet more beautiful the sparks of greatness and nobleness that had just revived.

No doubt we shared the same thoughts, for I believe that blindness renders intellectual communications much more rapid, by preventing the attention from flitting away to exterior objects. The proof of our sympathy was not long in showing itself. Facino Cane stopped playing, rose from his seat, came to me, and said one word—

"*Sortons!*"

The effect it produced on me was like an electric douche. I gave him my arm and we went out.

When we were in the street, he said to me: "Will you take me to Venice, will you be my guide, will you have faith in me? You shall be richer than the ten richest houses in Amsterdam or London, richer than the Rothschilds, as rich as the Thousand-and-One Nights."

I thought the man was mad; but there was a power in his voice which I obeyed. I let him guide me; he led me toward the trenches of the Bastille, as if he had eyes. He sat down on a very lonely place, where the bridge connecting the Canal Saint Martin and the Seine has since been built. I placed myself on another stone in front of the old man, his white hair glistened like threads of silver in the moonlight. The silence, scarcely broken by the stormy sounds which reached us from the boulevards, the purity of the night—everything—combined to render the scene really fantastic.

"You speak of millions to a young man, and do you think he would hesitate to endure a thousand evils in order to obtain them! But you are not making fun of me?"

"May I die without confession," he said passionately, "if what I am going to tell you is not true. I
was twenty—just as you are now—I was rich, handsome, and a noble. I began with the greatest of all
madness—Love. I loved as men love no longer; I
even hid in a chest at the risk of being stabbed to death
in it, without having received anything more than the
promise of a kiss. To die for her seemed to me life
itself. In 1760 I became enamored of one of the
Vendramini, a woman of eighteen, who was married
to a Sagredo, one of the richest senators, a man of
thirty, and mad about his wife. My mistress and I
were as innocent as two cherubim when *il sposo* surprised us talking of love. I was unarmed; he missed
me; I leaped upon him and strangled him with my
two hands, wringing his neck like a chicken. I wanted
to fly with Bianca, but she would not follow me. It
was so like a woman! I went alone. I was condemned, and my goods were confiscated to the benefit
of my heirs; but I had rolled up and carried away with
me five pictures by Tizian, my diamonds, and all my
gold. I went to Milan, where I was left in peace, as
my affair did not concern the State."

"Just one remark before I go," he said, after a
pause. "Whether the fancies of a woman when she
conceives, or while she is pregnant, influence her child
or not, it is certain that my mother during her preg-
nancy had a passion for gold. I have a monomania
for gold, the satisfaction of which is so necessary to
my life that, in all situations I have found myself, I
have never been without gold upon me. I have a constant mania for gold. When I was young I always

wore jewelry, and always carried two or three hundred ducats about with me."

As he said these words he drew two ducats out of his pocket and showed them to me.

"I feel gold. Although I am blind, I stop before jewellers' shops. This passion ruined me. I became a gambler for the sake of gambling with gold. I was not a cheat, I was cheated; I ruined myself. When I had no fortune left I was seized by a mad longing to see Bianca; I returned to Venice in secret, found her again, and was happy for six months, hidden in her house and supported by her. I used to have delicious dreams of ending my life like this. She was courted by the *Provedittore;* he divined he had a rival. In Italy we have an instinct for them. The dastard played the spy upon us and caught us in bed. You may guess how fierce the fight was. I did not kill him, but I wounded him very severely. This event shattered our happiness; since then I have never found another Bianca. I have enjoyed great favors; I have lived at the Court of Louis XV. among the most celebrated women; I have not found anywhere the noble qualities, the charms, the love, of my dear Venetian. The *Provedittore* had his servants with him; he called them; they surrounded the palace, and entered. I defended myself that I might die before Bianca's eyes—she helped me to kill the *Provedittore.* Before, this woman had refused to fly with me; but after six months of happiness she was ready to die on my body, and received several wounds. I was taken in a large mantle which they threw over me; they rolled me up in it, carried me away in a gondola, and put me in   a cell in the dun-

geon. I was twenty-two. I held the stump of my
sword so tight that they would have been obliged to
cut off my wrist in order to take it away. By a strange
chance, or rather inspired by some instinct of precaution, I hid this fragment of metal in a corner as a
thing of possible use to me. My wounds were dressed,
none of them were mortal; at twenty-two a man recovers from anything. I was to die by beheading. I
feigned sickness to gain time. I believed I was in a
cell bordering on the canal; my project was to escape
by undermining the wall, and risk being drowned by
swimming across the canal. My hopes were founded
on the following calculations: Every time the jailer
brought me food I read the notices fastened on the
walls, such as—*The Palace; The Canal; The Subter-
ranean Prisons.* Thus I succeeded in making out a
plan which caused me some little apprehension, but
was to be explained by the actual state of the ducal
palace, which has never been finished. With that
genius which the longing to recover one's liberty gives
a man, I succeeded, by feeling the surface of a stone
with the tips of my fingers, in deciphering an Arabic
inscription, by which the author of the work warned
his successors that he had dislodged two stones of the
last course of masonry and dug eleven feet under-
ground. To continue his work, it would be necessary
to spread the fragments of stone and mortar caused by
the work of excavation over the floor of the cell itself.
Even if the jailers and *Inquisatori* had not felt satisfied, that, from the construction of the building, it only
needed an external guard, the arrangement of the cells,
in which was a descent of several steps, allowed the
floor to be gradually raised without attracting the

jailer's notice. This immense labor had been super-
fluous at least for the unknown person who had undertaken it; its incompletion was an evidence of his death.
That his exertions might not be lost forever, it was
necessary that a prisoner should know Arabic. Now I
had studied the oriental languages at the Armenian
convent. A sentence written behind the stone told the
unhappy man's fate; he had died a victim to his immense wealth, which was coveted and seized by Venice.
It would require a month to arrive at any result.
While I worked, and during those moments when I
was prostrate with fatigue, I heard the sound of gold;
I saw gold before me; I was dazzled by diamonds!
Now, listen! One night my blunt sword touched
wood. I sharpened the stump, and began to make a
hole in the wood. In order to work, I used to crawl on
my belly like a snake. I stripped myself and worked
like a mole, with my hands in front, and using the rock
itself as a fulcrum. Two nights before the day I was
to appear before my judges, I determined to make one
last effort during the night. I bored through the
wood, and my sword touched nothing. You can
imagine my amazement when I put my eye to the hole!
I was in the panelled roof of a cellar, in which a dim
light enabled me to see a heap of gold. In the cellar
were the Doge and one of the Ten. I could hear their
voices. I learned from their conversation that here
was the secret treasure of the Republic, the gifts of the
Doges and the reserves of booty called *The last hope of
Venice,* a certain proportion of the spoils of all expedi-
tions. I was saved! When the jailer came, I proposed
to him to help me to escape and to fly with me, taking
with us everything we could get. He had no cause

to hesitate; he agreed. A ship was about to set sail for the Levant; every precaution was taken. I dictated a plan to my accomplice, and Bianca assisted in carrying it out. To avoid giving the alarm, Bianca was to join us at Smyrna. In one night we enlarged the hole and descended into the secret treasury of Venice. What a night it was! I saw four tons full of gold. In the first chamber the silver was piled up in two even heaps, leaving a path between them by which to pass through the room; the coins formed banks, which covered the walls to the height of five feet. I thought the jailer would have gone mad; he sang, he leaped, he laughed, he gambolled about in the gold. I threatened to throttle him if he wasted the time or made a noise. In his delight he did not at first see a table where the diamonds were. I swooped down upon it so skilfully that I was able to fill my sailor's vest and the pockets of my pantaloons. My God! I did not take a third part. Under this table were ingots of gold. I persuaded my companion to fill as many sacks as we could carry with gold, pointing out to him that it was the only way to avoid being discovered in a foreign country. The pearls, jewelry, and diamonds, I told him, would lead to our being found out. In spite of our greed, we could not take more than two thousand *livres* of gold, and this necessitated six journeys across the prison to the gondola. The sentinel at the water-gate had been bought with a bag containing ten *livres* of gold; as for the two gondoliers, they believed they were serving the Republic. At daybreak we departed. When we were out at sea and I thought of that night, when I recalled the sensations which I had experienced, and seemed to see again that immense

treasure, of which I calculated I must have left thirty
millions in silver and twenty millions in gold, besides
several millions in diamonds, pearls, and rubies; a feeling of madness rose within me; I had gold fever. We
were landed at Smyrna, and immediately re-embarked
for France. As we were going on board the French
vessel, God did me the favor of relieving me of my accomplice. At the moment I did not think of all the
bearings of this mishap; I was greatly rejoiced at it.
We were so completely enervated that we remained in
a state of torpor, without speaking, waiting until we
were in a place of safety to play our parts at our ease.
It is not to be wondered at that the fellow's head had
been turned. You will see how God punished me. I
did not consider myself safe until I had disposed of
two-thirds of my diamonds in London and Amsterdam, and realized my gold dust in negotiable species.
For five years I hid myself in Madrid; then in 1770 I
came to Paris under a Spanish name, and lived in the
most brilliant style.

"Bianca was dead.

"In the midst of my pleasures, when I was enjoying
a fortune of six millions, I was struck with blindness.
I concluded that this infirmity was the result of my so-
journ in the prison and my labors in the dark, if indeed my faculty for seeing gold did not imply an abuse
of the powers of vision and predestine me to lose my
eyes. At this time I loved a woman to whom I had
resolved to link my fate. I had told her the secret of
my name; she belonged to a powerful family, and I
had every hope from the favor shown me by Louis
XV.; she was a friend of Madame du Barry. I had
put my trust in this woman; she advised me to consult

a famous oculist in London; then, after staying in the town for some months, she deserted me in Hyde Park, robbing me of the whole of my fortune and leaving me without resources. I was obliged to conceal my name, for it would have exposed me to the vengeance of Venice. I could not invoke any one's help; I was afraid of Venice. The spies whom this woman ´had attached to my person had made capital out of my blindness. I spare you the history of adventures worthy of Gil Blas. Your Revolution came; I was obliged to enter at Les Quinze-Vingts; this creature got me admitted after having kept me for two years at Bicêtre as insane. I have never been able to kill her, I could not see to, and I was too poor to pay another hand. If, before I lost Benedetto Carpi, my jailer, I had consulted him on the situation of my cell, I should have been able to find the treasury again and return to Venice when the Republic was abolished by Napoleon. However, in spite of my blindness, let us go to Venice! I will find the door of the prison, I shall see the gold through the walls, I shall feel it where it lies buried beneath the waters; for the events which overturned the power of Venice are such that the secret of the treasury must have died with Vendramino, the brother of Bianca, a Doge who, I hoped, would have made my peace with the Ten. I addressed notes to the First Consul, I proposed an agreement with the Emperor of Austria; every one treated me as a madman! Come, let us start for Venice, let us start beggars; we shall come back millionaires; we will buy back my property, and you shall be my heir, you shall be Prince of Varese."

I was thunderstruck at this confidence, at the sight

of that white head; before the black waters of the trenches of the Bastille sleeping as still as the canals of Venice, it assumed in my imagination the proportions of a poem. I gave no answer. Facino Cane no doubt believed that I judged him, like all the rest, with disdainful pity; he made a gesture expressive of all the philosophy of despair. Perhaps his story had carried him back to those happy days at Venice; he seized his clarionet and played with the deepest pathos a Venetian song, a barcarolle in which he recovered all his first talent—the talent which was his when he was a patrician and in love. It was as it were a *Super flumina Babylonis*. My eyes filled with tears.

If some belated passers-by chanced to be walking along le boulevard Bourdon, I dare say they stopped to listen to this last prayer of the exile, this last regret of a lost name, mingled with memories of Bianca. But gold soon got the mastery again, and its fatal passion quenched the glimmering of youth.

"That treasure!" he said; "I see it always, waking and in my dreams; I take my walks there, the diamonds sparkle, I am not so blind as you think; gold and diamonds lighten my night, the night of the last Facino Cane, for my title passes to the Memmi. Good God! the murderer's punishment has begun betimes! *Ave Maria!*" . .

He recited some prayers which I could not hear.

"We will go to Venice," I exclaimed, as he was getting up.

"Then I have found my man," he cried, with a glow upon his face. I gave him my arm and led him back; at the door of Les Quinze-Vingts he pressed my hand; just then some of the people from the wedding were

going home, shouting enough to blow one's head off.
"We will start to-morrow?" said the old man.
"As soon as we have got some money."
"But we can go on foot; I will ask alms—I am
strong, and when a man sees gold before him he is
strong."

Facino Cane died during the winter after lingering
for two months. The poor man had caught a chill.

DOOMED TO LIVE

DOOMED TO LIVE

THE clock of the little town of Menda had just struck midnight. At this moment a young French officer was leaning on the parapet of a long terrace which bounded the gardens of the castle. He seemed plunged in the deepest thought—a circumstance unusual amid the thoughtlessness of military life; but it must be owned that never were the hour, the night, and the place more propitious to meditation. The beautiful Spanish sky stretched out its azure dome above his head. The glittering stars and the soft moonlight lit up a charming valley that unfolded all its beauties at his feet. Leaning against a blossoming orange tree, he could see, a hundred feet below him, the town of Menda, which seemed to have been placed for shelter from the north winds at the foot of the rock on which the castle was built. As he turned his head he could see the sea, framing the landscape with a broad silver sheet of glistening water. The castle was a blaze of light. The mirth and movement of a ball, the music of the orchestra, the laughter of the officers and their partners in the dance, were borne to him mingled with the distant murmur of the waves. The freshness of the night imparted a sort of energy to his limbs, weary with the heat of the day. Above all, the gardens were planted with trees so aromatic, and flowers so fragrant,

175

that the young man stood plunged, as it were, in a bath of perfumes.

The castle cf Menda belonged to a Spanish grandee, then living there with his family. During the whole of the evening his eldest daughter had looked at the officer with an interest so tinged with sadness that the sentiment of compassion thus expressed by the Spaniard might well call up a reverie in the Frenchman's mind.

Clara was beautiful, and although she had three brothers and a sister, the wealth of the Marques de Leganes seemed great enough for Victor Marchand to believe that the young lady would have a rich dowry. But how dare he hope that the most bigoted old hidalgo in all Spain would ever give his daughter to the son of a Parisian grocer? Besides, the French were hated. The Marques was suspected by General Gautier, who governed the province, of planning a revolt in favor of Ferdinand VII. For this reason the battalion commanded by Victor Marchand had been cantonned in the little town of Menda, to hold the neighboring hamlets, which were dependent on the Marques, in check. Recent despatches from Marshal Ney had given ground for fear that the English would shortly land on the coast, and had indicated the Marques as a man who carried on communication with the cabinet of London.

In spite, therefore, of the welcome which the Spaniard had given him and his soldiers, the young officer Victor Marchand remained constantly on his guard. As he was directing his steps toward the terrace whither he had come to examine the state of the town and the country districts entrusted to his care, he debated how he ought to interpret the friendliness which the Marques had unceasingly shown him, and how the tranquillity of the country could be reconciled with his General's uneasiness. But in one moment these thoughts were driven from his mind by a feeling of caution and well-grounded curiosity. He had just perceived a considerable number of lights in the town. In spite of the day being the Feast of St. James, he had given orders, that very morning, that all lights should be extinguished at the hour prescribed by his regulations, the castle alone being excepted from this order. He could plainly see, here and there, the gleam of his soldiers' bayonets at their accustomed posts; but there was a solemnity in the silence, and nothing to suggest that the Spaniards were a prey to the excitement of a festival. After having sought to explain the offence of which the inhabitants were guilty, the mystery appeared all the more unaccountable to him, because he had left officers in charge of the night police and the rounds.' With all the impetuosity of youth, he was just about to leap through a breach and descend the rocks in haste, and thus arrive more quickly than by the ordinary road at a small outpost placed at the entrance of the town nearest to the castle, when a faint sound stopped him. He thought he heard the light footfall of a woman upon the gravel walk. He turned his head and saw nothing; but his gaze was arrested by the extraordinary brightness of the sea. All of a sudden he beheld a sight so portentous that he stood dumbfounded; he thought that his senses deceived him. In the far distance he could distinguish sails gleaming white in the moonlight. He trembled and tried to convince himself that this vision was an optical illusion, merely the fantastic effect of the moon on the waves. At this moment a hoarse voice pronounced his name. He looked toward the breach, and saw slowly rising above it the head of the soldier whom he had ordered to accompany him to the castle.

"Is that you, Commandant?"

"Yes; what do you want?" replied the young man in a low voice. A sort of presentiment warned him to be cautious.

"Those rascals down there are stirring like worms. I have hurried, with your leave, to tell you my own little observations."

"Go on," said Victor Marchand.

"I have just followed a man from the castle who came in this direction with a lantern in his hand. A lantern's a frightfully suspicious thing. I don't fancy it was tapers my fine Catholic was going to light at this time of night. 'They want to eat us, body and bones!' says I to myself; so I went on his track to reconnoiter. There, on a ledge of rock, not three paces from here, I discovered a great heap of faggots."

Suddenly a terrible shriek ran through the town, and cut the soldier short. At the same instant a gleam of light flashed before the Commandant. The poor grenadier received a ball in the head and fell. A fire of straw and dry wood burst into flame like a house on fire, not ten paces from the young man. The sound of the instruments and the laughter ceased in the ball-room. The silence of death, broken only by groans, had suddenly succeeded to the noises and music of the feast. The fire of a cannon roared over the surface of the sea. Cold sweat trickled down the young offi-

cer's forehead; he had no sword. He understood that
his men had been slaughtered, and the English were
about to disembark. If he lived he saw himself dis-
honored, summoned before a council of war. Then
he measured with his eyes the depth of the valley. He
sprang forward, when just at that moment his hand
was seized by the hand of Clara.

"Fly!" said she; "my brothers are following to kill
you. Down yonder at the foot of the rock you will
find Juanito's andalusian. Quick!"

The young man looked at her for a moment stupefied. She pushed him on; then, obeying the instinct
of self-preservation which never forsakes even the
bravest man, he rushed down the park in the direction
she had indicated. He leaped from rock to rock,
where only the goats had ever trod before; he heard
Clara crying out to her brothers to pursue him; he
heard the footsteps of the assassins; he heard the balls
of several discharges whistle about his ears; but he
reached the valley, he found the horse, mounted, and
disappeared swift as lightning. In a few hours he
arrived at the quarters occupied by General Gautier.
He found him at dinner with his staff.

"I bring you my life in my hand!" cried the Commandant, his face pale and haggard.

He sat down and related the horrible disaster. A
dreadful silence greeted his story.

"You appear to me to be more unfortunate than
criminal," said the terrible General at last. "You are
not accountable for the crimes of the Spaniards, and
unless the Marshal decides otherwise, I acquit you."

These words could give the unfortunate officer but
slight consolation.

"But when the Emperor hears of it!" he exclaimed.
"He will want to have you shot," said the General.
"However—— But we will talk no more about it,"
he added severely, "except how we are to take such a
revenge as will strike wholesome fear upon this country, where they carry on war like savages."

One hour afterward, a whole regiment, a detachment of cavalry, and a convoy of artillery were on the
road. The General and Victor marched at the head of
the column. The soldiers, informed of the massacre
of their comrades, were filled with extraordinary fury.
The distance which separated the town of Menda from
the general quarters was passed with marvellous rapid-
ity. On the road the General found whole villages
under arms. Each of these wretched townships was
surrounded and their inhabitants decimated.

By some inexplicable fatality, the English ships
stood off instead of advancing. It was known afterward that these vessels had outstripped the rest of the
transports and only carried artillery. Thus the town
of Menda, deprived of the defenders she was expecting, and which the sight of the English vessels had
seemed to assure, was surrounded by the French troops
almost without striking a blow. The inhabitants,
seized with terror, offered to surrender at discretion.
Then followed one of those instances of devotion not
rare in the Peninsula. The assassins of the French,
foreseeing, from the cruelty of the General, that
Menda would probably be given over to the flames and
the whole population put to the sword, offered to de-
nounce themselves. The General accepted this offer,
inserting as a condition that the inhabitants of the
castle, from the lowest valet to the Marques himself,

should be placed in his hands. This capitulation agreed upon, the General promised to pardon the rest of the population and to prevent his soldiers from pillaging or setting fire to the town. An enormous contribution was exacted, and the richest inhabitants gave themselves up as hostages to guarantee the payment, which was to be accomplished within twenty-four hours.

The General took all precautions necessary for the safety of his troops, provided for the defence of the country, and refused to lodge his men in the houses. After having formed a camp, he went up and took military possession of the castle. The members of the family of Leganes and the servants were gagged, and shut up in the great hall where the ball had taken place, and closely watched. The windows of the apartment afforded a full view of the terrace which commanded the town. The staff was established in a neighboring gallery, and the General proceeded at once to hold a council of war on the measures to be taken for opposing the debarkation. After having despatched an aide-de-camp to Marshal Ney, with orders to plant batteries along the coast, the General and his staff turned their attention to the prisoners. Two hundred Spaniards, whom the inhabitants had surrendered, were shot down then and there upon the terrace. After this military execution the General ordered as many gallows to be erected on the terrace as there were prisoners in the hall of the castle, and the town executioner to be brought. Victor Marchand made use of the time from then until dinner to go and visit the prisoners. He soon returned to the General.

"I have come," said he, in a voice broken with emotion, "to ask you a favor."

"You?" said the General, in a tone of bitter irony.

"Alas!" replied Victor, "it is but a melancholy errand that I am come on. The Marques has seen the gallows being erected, and expresses a hope that you will change the mode of execution for his family; he entreats you to have the nobles beheaded."

"So be it!" said the General.

"They further ask you to allow them the last consolations of religion, and to take off their bonds; they promise not to attempt to escape."

"I consent," said the General; "but you must be answerable for them."

"The old man also offers you the whole of his fortune if you will pardon his young son."

"Really!" said the General. "His goods already belong to King Joseph; he is under arrest." His brow contracted scornfully, then he added: "I will go beyond what they ask. I understand now the importance of the last request. Well, let him buy the eternity of his name, but Spain shall remember forever his treachery and its punishment. I give up the fortune and his life to whichever of his sons will fulfill the office of executioner. Go, and do not speak to me of it again."

Dinner was ready, and the officers sat down to table to satisfy appetites sharpened by fatigue.

One of them only, Victor Marchand, was not present at the banquet. He hesitated for a long time before he entered the room. The haughty family of Leganes were in their agony. He glanced sadly at the scene before him; in this very room, only the night before, he had watched the fair heads of those two young girls and those three youths as they circled in the excitement of the dance. He shuddered when he thought how soon they must fall, struck off by the sword of the headsman. Fastened to their gilded chairs, the father and mother, their three sons, and their two young daughters, sat absolutely motionless. Eight serving-men stood upright before them, their hands bound behind their backs. These fifteen persons looked at each other gravely, their eyes scarcely betraying the thoughts that surged within them. Only profound resignation and regret for the failure of their enterprise left any mark upon the features of some of them. The soldiers stood likewise motionless, looking at them, and respecting the affliction of their cruel enemies. An expression of curiosity lit up their faces when Victor appeared. He gave the order to unbind the condemned, and went himself to loose the cords which fastened Clara to her chair. She smiled sadly. He could not refrain from touching her arm, and looking with admiring eyes at her black locks and graceful figure. She was a true Spaniard; she had the Spanish complexion and the Spanish eyes, with their long curled lashes and pupils blacker than the raven's wing.

"Have you been successful?" she said, smiling upon him mournfully with somewhat of the charm of girlhood still lingering in her eyes.

Victor could not suppress a groan. He looked one after the other at Clara and her three brothers. One, the eldest, was aged thirty; he was small, even somewhat ill made, with a proud disdainful look, but there was a certain nobleness in his bearing; he seemed no stranger to that delicacy of feeling which elsewhere has rendered the chivalry of Spain so famous. His name was Juanito. The second, Felipe, was aged about twenty; he was like Clara. The youngest was eight, Manuel; a painter would have found in his features a trace of that Roman steadfastness which David had given to children's faces in his episodes of the Republic. The old Marques, his head still covered with white locks, seemed to have come forth from a picture of Murillo. The young officer shook his head. When he looked at them, he was hopeless that he would ever see the bargain proposed by the General accepted by any of the four; nevertheless he ventured to impart it to Clara. At first she shuddered, Spaniard though she was; then, immediately recovering her calm demeanor, she went and knelt down before her father.

"Father," she said, "make Juanito swear to obey faithfully any orders that you give him, and we shall be content."

The Marquesa trembled with hope; but when she leaned toward her husband, and heard—she who was a mother—the horrible confidence whispered by Clara, she swooned away. Juanito understood all; he leaped up like a lion in its cage. After obtaining an assurance of perfect submission from the Marques, Victor took upon himself to send away the soldiers. The servants were led out, handed over to the executioner, and hanged. When the family had no guard but Victor to watch them, the old father rose and said, "Juanito."

Juanito made no answer, except by a movement of the head, equivalent to a refusal; then he fell back in his seat, and stared at his parents with eyes dry and terrible to look upon. Clara went and sat on his knee, put her arm around his neck, and kissed his eyelids.

"My dear Juanito," she said gaily, "if thou didst only know how sweet death would be to me if it were given by thee, I should not have to endure the odious touch of the headsman's hands. Thou wilt cure me of the woes that were in store for me—and, dear Juanito, thou couldst not bear to see me belong to another, well——" Her soft eyes cast one look of fire at Victor, as if to awaken in Juanito's heart his horror of the French.

"Have courage," said his brother Felipe, "or else our race, which has almost given kings to Spain, will be extinct."

Suddenly Clara rose, the group which had formed round Juanito separated, and his son, dutiful in his disobedience, saw his aged father standing before him, and heard him cry in a solemn voice, "Juanito, I command thee."

The young Count remained motionless. His father fell on his knees before him; Clara, Manuel, and Felipe did the same instinctively. They all stretched out their hands to him as to one who was to save their family from oblivion; they seemed to repeat their father's words—"My son, hast thou lost the energy, the true chivalry of Spain? How long wilt thou leave thy father on his knees? What right hast thou to think of thine own life and its suffering? Madam, is this a son of mine?" continued the old man, turning to his wife.

"He consents," cried she, in despair. She saw a movement in Juanito's eyelids, and she alone understood its meaning.

Mariquita, the second daughter, still knelt on her knees, and clasped her mother in her fragile arms; her little brother Manuel, seeing her weeping·hot tears, began to chide her. At this moment the almoner of the castle came in; he was immediately surrounded by the rest of the family and brought to Juanito. Victor could bear this scene no longer; he made a sign to Clara, and hastened away to make one last effort with the General. He found him in high good-humor in the middle of the banquet, drinking with his officers; they were beginning to make merry.

An hour later a hundred of the principal inhabitants of Menda came up. to the terrace, in obedience to the General's orders, to witness the execution of the family of Leganes. A detachment of soldiers was drawn up to keep back the Spanish burghers who were ranged under the gallows on which the servants of the Marques still hung. The feet of these martyrs almost touched their; heads. Thirty yards from them a block had been set up, and by it gleamed a scimitar. The headsman also was present, in case of Juanito's refusal. Presently, in the midst of the profoundest silence, the Spaniards heard the footsteps of several persons approaching, the measured tread of a company of soldiers, and the faint clinking of their muskets. These diverse sounds were mingled with the merriment of the officers' banquet; just as before it was the music of the dance which had concealed preparations for a treacherous massacre. All eyes were turned toward the castle; the noble family was seen advancing with incredible dignity. Every face was calm and serene; one man only leaned, pale and haggard, on the arm of the Priest. Upon this man he lavished all the consolations of religion—upon the only one of them doomed to live. The executioner understood, as did all the rest, that for that day Juanito had undertaken the office himself. The aged Marques and his wife, Clara, Mariquita, and their two brothers, came and knelt down a few steps from the fatal spot. Juanito was led thither by the Priest. As he approached the block the executioner touched him by the sleeve and drew him aside, probably to give him certain instructions.

The Confessor placed the victims in such a position that they could not see the executioner; but like true Spaniards, they knelt erect without a sign of emotion.

Clara was the first to spring forward to her brother. "Juanito," she said, "have pity on my faint-heartedness; begin with me."

At that moment they heard the footstep of a man running at full speed, and Victor arrived on the tragic scene. Clara was already on her knees, already her white neck seemed to invite the edge of the scimitar. A deadly pallor fell upon the officer, but he still found strength to run on.

"The General grants thee thy life if thou wilt marry me," he said to her in a low voice.

The Spaniard cast a look of proud disdain on the officer. "Strike, Juanito," she said, in a voice of profound meaning.

Her head rolled at Victor's feet. When the Marquesa heard the sound a convulsive start escaped her; this was the only sign of her affliction.

"Am I placed right so, dear Juanito?" little Manuel asked his brother.

"Ah, thou weepest, Mariquita!" said Juanito to his sister.

"Yes," answered the girl; "I was thinking of thee, my poor Juanito; thou wilt be so unhappy without us."

At length the noble figure of the Marques appeared. He looked at the blood of his children; then he turned to the spectators, who stood mute and motionless before him. He stretched out his hands to Juanito, and said in a firm voice: "Spaniards, I give my son a father's blessing. Now, Marques, strike without fear, as thou art without fault."

But when Juanito saw his mother approach, supported by the Confessor, he groaned aloud. "She fed me at her own breast." His cry seemed to tear a shout of horror from the lips of the crowd. At this terrible sound the noise of the banquet and the laughter and merry-making of the officers died away. The Marquesa comprehended that Juanito's courage was exhausted. With one leap she had thrown herself over the balustrade, and her head was dashed to pieces against the rocks below. A shout of admiration burst forth. Juanito fell to the ground in a swoon.

"Marchand has just been telling me something about this execution," said a half-drunken officer. "I'll warrant, General, it wasn't by your orders that——"

"Have you forgotten, Messieurs," cried General Gautier, "that during the next month there will be five hundred French families in tears, and that we are in Spain? Do you wish to leave your bones here?"

After this speech there was not a man, not even a sub-lieutenant, who dared to empty his glass.

In spite of the respect with which he is surrounded —in spite of the title of El Verdugo (the executioner), bestowed upon him as a title of nobility by the King of

Spain—the Marques de Leganes is a prey to melancholy. He lives in solitude, and is rarely seen. Overwhelmed with the load of his glorious crime, he seems only to wait the birth of a second son, impatient to seek again the company of those Shades who are about his path continually.

AN ACCURSED HOUSE

AN ACCURSED HOUSE

(A Story related by Horace Bianchon)

On the banks of the Loire, about a stone's throw from Vendôme, stands an old brown house, with a very steep roof. Even the stinking tanyards and the wretched taverns found on the outskirts of almost all small towns have no place here; the isolation is complete. At the back of this dwelling, leading down to the bank of the river, is a garden. The box, once clipped to mark the walks, grows now as it will; some willows sprung from the Loire have formed a boundary with their rapid growth, and almost hide the house; plants which we call weeds make the sloping bank beautiful with their luxuriant growth; the fruit trees, unpruned for ten years, form a thicket with their suckers, and yield no harvest; the espaliers have grown as bushy as a hedge of elms; paths once sanded are covered with purslain—or rather, of the paths themselves there is left no trace. From the brow of the hill hang, as it were, the ruins of the ancient castle of the Dukes of Vendôme; it is the only place whence the eye can penetrate into this retreat.

It is said that this strip of land was once—at a date difficult to fix exactly—the delight of a gentleman who spent his time in the cultivation of roses and tulips;

in fact, in horticulture generally, especially devoting himself to the rarer fruits. An arbor—or rather, the ruins of one—is still visible, and in it a table which time has not yet entirely destroyed. The sight of this garden which is no more reminds one of the negative enjoyment of life spent peacefully in the country, just as one guesses at the story of a successful merchant from the epitaph on his tomb. To complete the sad and sweet thoughts which fasten here upon the soul, one of the walls bears a sun dial inscribed with this legend, "Ultimam cogita"—such is the reminder of its somewhat matter-of-fact Christianity. The roofs of this house are utterly ruinous, the shutters are always closed, the balconies full of swallows' nests, the doors forever shut; tall grasses etch with their green outline the cracks in the pavement, the bolts are red with rust. Summer and winter the sun and the moon and the snow have cracked the wood and shrunk the planks and gnawed away the paint. Here silence and gloom hold their untroubled sway, only birds, and cats, and rats, and mice, and martins roam here unmolested, and fight their battles, and prey upon each other. Over all an invisible hand has written the one word—mystery.

If you were driven by your curiosity to go round and look at the house on the other side, from the road, you would notice a wide-arched door, through which the children of the neighborhood have made plenty of peep-holes—I learned afterward that this door had been past repair ten years before—and through these irregular chinks you could see the perfect harmony there is between the garden front and the front looking on to the courtyard. Here is the same reign of

lisorder—the flagstones are edged with tufts of grass,
:normous cracks run like furrows over the walls, the
)lackened coping is interlaced with festoons of countess wall plants, the stones of the steps are unjointed,
he gutters are broken, the cord of the bell has rotted
iway. Has fire from heaven passed through this
lwelling? Did some tribunal decree that this habita-
:ion should be sown with salt? Has man betrayed
France in this place—insulted God? These are the
juestions one asks here; only the reptiles writhe and
inswer not. This empty, desolate house is a vast
:nigma, and no man knows the clue. It was formerly
i small manor, and bears the name of La Grande
Brétèche. During my stay at Vendôme, where Despleins had left me to take care of a rich patient, the
sight of this strange dwelling became one of my keen-
est pleasures. It was more than a ruin; to a ruin are
attached at least some remembrances of incontestable
authenticity; but this habitation, still standing, slowly
decaying beneath an avenging hand, held within it a
secret—a thought unknown. At the least its mere
existence was the sign of some strange caprice. Many
a time of an evening I resolutely approached the now
wild hedgerow which protected the enclosure. I braved
the tearing thorns, and trod this garden without an
owner, and entered this possession no longer public or
private. I stayed there whole hours gazing upon its
disorder. Not even for the sake of learning the story
—which I felt certain would give an explanation of
this strange scene—would I have made a single inquiry
of any of the gossips of Vendôme. There I composed
charming romances; I gave myself up to little de-
bauches of melancholy which delighted my heart. If I

had known the cause of this desertion (perhaps a commonplace story enough), I should have lost the intoxication of these my unpublished poems. To me this retreat represented the most varied pictures of human life clouded by misery. Now it had the air of a cloister without inmates; now the peace of a cemetery without the dead and all their chattering epitaphs; one day it was a lazar-house, the next the Palace of the Atridae; but above all it was the country with its hour glass existence, and its conventional ideas. I have often wept, I never laughed there. More than once I felt an involuntary terror when I heard above my head the dull whir of the wings of some belated wood dove. There the soil is so dank you must defy the lizards and vipers and frogs that walk abroad in all the wild liberty of Nature. Above all, you must not mind the cold; at certain moments you feel as though a mantle of ice were cast upon your shoulders, like the commandant's hand upon Don Juan's neck.

One evening, just at the moment I was finishing a tragedy by which I was explaining to myself the phenomenon of this sort of woe in effigy, the wind turned an old rusty weathercock, and the cry it gave forth sounded like a groan bursting from the depth of the house; I shivered with terror.

I returned to my inn overpowered with gloomy thoughts. When I had supped, my hostess came with a mysterious air into my room, and said, "Monsieur, Monsieur Regnault is here." "Who is Monsieur Regnault?" "Why! does not Monsieur know Monsieur Regnault? Ah, that's very odd," she said, and went away. Suddenly I saw before me a long, lean man; he entered the room like a ram gathering itself up to

butt at a rival; he presented a receding forehead, a
little pointed head, and a sallow face, not unlike a glass
of dirty water; he might have passed for a ministerial
beadle. This man, who was quite unknown to me,
wore a black coat, very much worn at the seams, but
he had a diamond in the bosom of his shirt and gold
rings in his ears.

"Monsieur, whom have I the honor of addressing?"
said I. He seated himself on a chair, arranged himself
before my fire, placed his hat on my table, rubbed his
hands together and said, "Ah! it's very cold. Monsieur, I am Monsieur Regnault." I bowed, saying to
myself, "Il bondo cani! let's see."

"I am," said he, "a notary in Vendôme." "I am
charmed to hear it, Monsieur," said I, "but I am not in
a position to make a will, for reasons known to myself." "Just one moment!" he replied, raising his hand
as if to impose silence. "Allow me, Monsieur, allow
me! I learn that you have occasionally gone to walk in
the garden of La Grande Brétèche." "Yes, Monsieur."
"Just one moment," said he, repeating his gesture;
"this of itself constitutes an actionable offence. Monsieur, I am come in the name and as executor under the
will of Madame, the late Comtesse de Merret, to request you to discontinue your visits. Just one moment!
I am no Turk; I do not wish to make a crime of it;
besides, you may very well be ignorant of the circumstances which oblige me to allow the finest mansion in
Vendôme to fall into ruins. However, Monsieur, you
appear to be a man of education, and you ought to
know that the laws forbid trespass on an enclosed estate under heavy penalties. A hedge is as good as a
wall. However, the state in which the house now

stands may serve as an excuse for your curiosity.
Nothing would give me more pleasure than to leave
you free to come and go as you please in the house;
but, charged as I am to carry out the wishes of the
testatrix, I have the honor, Monsieur, to request you
not to enter that garden again. Monsieur, since the
opening of the will I have not myself set foot in that
house, though it belongs—as I had the honor of in-
forming you—to the estate of Madame de Merret.
All we did was to make an inventory of the doors and
windows, in order to assess the taxes, which I pay an-
nually out of capital destined by the late Madame la
Comtesse for that purpose. Ah, my dear Monsieur,
her will made a great talk in Vendôme!"

Here the worthy man stopped to blow his nose. I
respected his loquacity, understanding perfectly that
the estate of Madame de Merret was the most important event in his life—his whole reputation, his
glory, his restoration. Then, after all, I must say
good-by to my fine reveries and romances. However, I
did not rebel against the satisfaction of learning the
truth in an official manner.

"Monsieur," I said, "would it be indiscreet if I
asked you the reason for this eccentricity?"

At these words a look expressing all the pleasure
of a man accustomed to mounting his hobby passed
over the notary's face. He pulled up his shirt collar
with a sort of self-satisfied air, took out his snuff-box,
opened it, offered me some snuff, and on my refusal
seized a large pinch himself. He was happy! The
man who has not got a hobby knows nothing of the
profit one can get out of life. A hobby is the exact
mean between passion and monomania. At this

moment I understood that charming expression of
Stern's in all its meaning. I had a complete idea of the
joy with which, by the aid of *Trim, Uncle Toby* be-
strode his charger.

"Monsieur," said Monsieur Regnault, "I was formerly senior clerk to Maitre Roguin, in Paris—an excellent office. Perhaps you have heard speak of it?
No! Well, a most unfortunate bankruptcy rendered
it notorious. Not having sufficient capital to carry on
business in Paris, considering the price to which practices went up in 1816, I came here and purchased the
office of my predecessor. I had relations here in Vendôme, among others a very rich aunt who gave me her
daughter in marriage. Monsieur," he continued after
a slight pause, "three months after I had been enrolled
before *Monseigneur le Garde des sceaux,* I was summoned one night just as I was going to bed (this was
before my marriage) by Madame la Comtesse de Merret to her chateau, le Chateau de Merret. Her lady's
maid, a fine young woman, now servant in this hotel,
was at my door in Madame le Comtesse's *calèche.* Ah!
just one moment! I ought to have told you, Monsieur,
that Monsieur le Comte de Merret had gone to Paris,
and died there two months before I came here. He
died miserably, having given himself up to every kind
of excess. You understand? The day of his de-
parture Madame la Comtesse had left La Grande
Brétèche and had it dismantled. Some people even de-
clare that she burned all the furniture, hangings—in
short, all the goods and chattels generally whatsoever
adorning the premises now in the tenancy of the said
sieur—(Dear me, what am I saying? Beg pardon, I
was thinking I was drawing up a lease.) Yes," he re-

peated, "they say she had them burned in the meadow
at Merret. Have you been to Merret, Monsieur?
No," said he, answering the question himself. "Ah!
it's a very fine place! For about three months before,
Monsieur le Comte and Madame la Comtesse had been
living in a strange manner. They no longer received
any one; Madame lived on the ground floor and Monsieur on the first story. After Madame la Comtesse
was left alone, she never showed herself again, except
at church; later she refused to see her friends who
came to visit her at home in her chateau. She was already very much changed when she left La Grande
Brétèche and went to live at Merret. The dear woman
(I say 'dear' because this diamond comes to me from
her, otherwise I never saw her but once). Well, the
good lady was very ill. No doubt she had given up
all hope of recovery, for she died without wishing any
doctors to be called in; indeed, many of our ladies here
thought that she was not quite right in the head. As
you may imagine then, Monsieur, my curiosity was
especially excited when I was informed that Madame
de Merret needed my assistance—and I was not the
only person who took interest in this story.

"Although it was late, the whole town knew that
same evening that I had gone to Merret. On the road
I addressed a few questions to the lady's maid, but her
answers were very vague; however, she told me that
the curé of Merret had come during the day and ad-
ministered the Last Sacraments to her mistress, and
that it seemed impossible that she could live through
the night. I arrived at the chateau about eleven o'clock.
I went up the great staircase; then, after traversing
vast, gloomy apartments, cold and damp enough for

the devil, I reached the principal bedchamber, where
Madame la Comtesse lay. After all the reports that
had been going about (I should never have finished,
Monsieur, if I were to repeat all the stories that are
told about her), I expected to see a sort of coquette.
Just fancy, I had the greatest difficulty to discover at
all where she was, in the great bed in which she lay.
True, she had one of those antique Argant lamps for
light, but the chamber was enormous, with an *ancien
régime frise* so covered with dust that the very sight
of it made one cough.   Ah! but you've not been to
Merret! Well! Monsieur, the bed is one of those old-
fashioned ones, with a high canopy trimmed with
figured chintz.   A small night table stood by the bedside, and I noticed on it a *Following of Christ,* which,
by the way, I afterward bought for my wife, as well
as the lamp; there was also a large couch for her confidential servant, and two chairs.   No fire, mind!
This was all the furniture; it wouldn't have filled ten
lines of an inventory.   Ah, *mon cher Monsieur,* if you
had seen, as I did then, this vast room, hung with
brown, you would have fancied you had been trans-
ported into a scene of a romance come true.   It was
icy, more than icy—funereal," he added, raising his
arm with a theatrical gesture and pausing.   "After
looking for some time and going close up to the bed,
at last I discovered Madame de Merret, thanks again
to the lamplight, which fell full upon her pillows.   Her
face was as yellow as wax; it was just like a pair of
clasped hands.   She had on a lace cap which showed
her beautiful hair; then, it was as white as thread.
She was sitting up, though she seemed to do so with
great difficulty.   Her great black eyes, dulled with

fever no doubt, and already almost dead, scarcely moved under the bones where the eyebrows are— here!" said he, pointing to the arch of his eyes. "Her brow was wet, her hands were fleshless, mere bones covered with a fine, tender skin; all her veins and muscles stood out prominently. She must have been very beautiful once, but at the moment I was seized with a feeling—I don't know how—at the sight of her. The people who laid her out said they had never seen a creature so utterly fleshless alive. She really was terrible to behold! Disease had made such ravages upon her she was nothing more than a phantom. Her lips were a livid purple; they seemed motionless even when she spoke. Although my profession takes me now and again to the bedsides of the dying in order to ascertain their last wishes, so that I am not unfamiliar with these scenes, yet I must say that the lamentations of the families and the agonies of the dying which I have witnessed are as nothing compared to this desolate and silent woman in her vast chateau. I could not hear the faintest sound, I could not even see the least movement of the bedclothes from the breathing of the sick woman; I too stood perfectly motionless, absorbed in looking at her, in a sort of stupor. I could fancy I was there now. At last her great eyes moved; she tried to lift her right hand, but it fell back on the bed, and these words passed out of her mouth like a sigh— her voice was a voice no more—'I have waited very impatiently for you.' Her cheeks flushed feverishly. It was a struggle for her to speak. 'Madame,' I said. She made me a sign to be silent, and at the same moment the old housekeeper rose from her couch and whispered in my ear: 'Do not speak; Madame la Comtesse

is not in a state to bear the least sound; if you spoke
you might agitate her.' I sat down. After a few
moments Madame de Merret gathered up all her remaining strength and moved her right arm; she put it
with immense difficulty under her bolster; then she
paused for a moment; then she made one last effort to
draw out her hand; she took out a sealed paper, and as
she did so the sweat fell in drops from her forehead.
'I entrust my will to you,' she said. 'Ah, my God, ah!'
This was all. She seized the crucifix which lay on her
bed, raised it quickly to her lips, and died. The expression of those motionless eyes makes me shudder
still; she must have suffered terribly! There was joy
in her last look, and the joy remained graven upon her
dead eyes. I took away the will with me; when it was
opened I found that Madame de Merret had named
me her executor. She bequeathed the whole of her
property to the hospital at Vendôme, with the exception of a few individual legacies. Her directions relative to La Grande Brétèche were as follows:—She directed me to leave the house for a period of fifty years
—reckoned from the day of her death—in the exact
state in which it should be found at the moment of her
decease; she forbade any entry into the apartments by
any person whatsoever, and also the least repair; she
even set aside the interest of a certain sum wherewith, if necessary, to engage keepers, in order to insure
the fulfilment of her intentions in their entirety. At
the expiration of this term of years, if the wishes of
the testatrix have been carried out, the house is to pass
to my heirs, for Monsieur is aware that notaries are
not allowed to accept a legacy; if they are not carried
out, La Grande Brétèche returns to the heirs-at-law,

with the charge that they are to fulfil the conditions
indicated in the codicil annexed to the will, which
codicil is not to be opened until the expiration of the
said fifty years. The will has never been disputed,
and so——;" at this word, and without finishing his
sentence, that oblong notary surveyed me with an air
of triumph, and I made him quite happy by addressing
him a few compliments. "Monsieur," I finished by
saying to him, "you have made such a vivid impression
upon me that I fancy I can see this dying woman paler
than her own sheets; her gleaming eyes made me
afraid; I shall dream of her to-night. But you will
have formed some conjectures concerning the disposi-
tions contained in this eccentric will?" "Monsieur,"
said he, with comic reserve, "I never allow myself to
judge of the conduct of persons who have honored me
with the gift of a diamond." I soon untied the tongue
of the scrupulous notary, and he communicated to me,
amid long digressions, all the observations made by
the profound politicians of both sexes whose judgments are law in Vendôme. But these observations
were so contradictory and so diffuse, that, in spite of
the interest which I took in this authentic history, I
very nearly fell asleep. The notary, no doubt accustomed to listen himself, and to make his clients and
fellow-townsmen listen too, to his dull voice and mo-
notonous intonation, began to triumph over my curiosity, when happily he got up to leave. "Ha, ha, Monsieur," said he, upon the staircase, "there are many
people who would like to be alive in forty-five years'
time, but—just one moment!" and he put the first
finger of his right hand to his nose, as if to say, "Pay
great attention to this," and said, in a sly way, "To

get as far as that, one must start before sixty." I was
drawn from my apathy by the last sally—the notary
thought it prodigiously witty; then I shut my door, sat
down in my armchair, and put my feet on the fire dogs
of the grate. I was soon deep in a romance à la Ann
Radcliffe, founded on the juridical hints given by
Monsieur Regnault. Presently my door, handled by
the dexterous hand of a woman, turned on its hinges;
my hostess came in, a good-humored, jovial woman,
who had missed her vocation; she was a Fleming, and
ought to have been born in a picture by Teniers.
"Well, Monsieur," said she, "I suppose Monsieur Regnault has been droning over his old story again about
La Grande Brétèche?" "Yes, he has, *mère* Lepas."
"What has he been telling you?" I repeated to her in
a few words the gloomy, chilling story of Madame de
Merret. After each sentence my hostess stretched out
her neck and looked at me with an innkeeper's own
shrewdness—a sort of happy mean between the instinct of a gendarme, the craft of a spy, and the
shiftiness of a shopkeeper. When I had finished I
added, "My dear *dame* Lepas! you seem to me to know
something more about it yourself, or else why should
you have come up to see me?" "No, on my word of
honor! as sure as my name's Lepas." "No, don't
swear to it; your eyes are big with a secret. You knew
Monsieur Merret; what was he like?" "Lord bless
you, Monsieur de Merret was a fine man; you never
got to the end of him, he was so long—a worthy
gentleman come from Picardie, but, as we say here,
'*Il avait la tête près du bonet.*' He paid everything
with ready money, so that he might never come to
words with any one; you see he was a bit quick! Our

ladies here all thought him very nice and pleasant."
"Because he was quick?" said I. "Likely enough,"
said she. "You may imagine, Monsieur, there must
have been a something about him, as they say, for
Madame de Merret to have married him. I don't want
to hurt the other ladies, but she was the richest and
prettiest young lady in all Vendôme; she had near on
twenty thousand *livres* a year. The whole town went
to see the wedding. The bride was a delicate, winning
creature—a real jewel of a wife. Ah! they made a
fine couple in their time!" "Were they happy together?" "Hm! perhaps they were and perhaps they
weren't, as far as one could tell; but you can imagine
they didn't hobnob with such as we. Madame de Merret made a good wife, and very kind. I dare say she
had a good bit to put up with at times from her husband's tantrums; but though he was a bit stern, we
liked him well enough. Bah! it's his quality that made
him like that; when a man's noble, you know——"
"Then there must certainly have been some catastrophe
for Monsieur and Madame de Merret to have separated so abruptly?" "I never said anything about a
catastrophe, Monsieur. I don't know anything about
it." "All right! Now I am certain that you do know
about it." "Well, Monsieur, I am going to tell you all
I know. When I saw Monsieur Regnault go up to see
you, I felt certain that he would talk to you about
Madame de Merret, with reference to La Grande
Brétèche. This put it into my head to consult Monsieur, for you seemed to me to be a comfortable man,
who would not betray a poor woman like me that has
never done harm to any one—and yet find myself tormented by my conscience. I have never up to now

dared to open my mouth about it to the people in this place: they're all a pack of gossips, with tongues like vinegar. In fact, Monsieur, I have never yet had a traveler stay in my house as long as you have, or any one to whom I could tell the history of the fifty thousand *francs*—" "My dear *dame* Lepas," I answered, checking the flow of her words, "if your confidence is of a nature to compromise me I wouldn't be burdened with it for all the world." "You needn't be afraid," said she, interrupting me, "you will see." This readiness made me think that I was not the only person to whom our good hostess had communicated the secret of which I was to be the sole depository; however, I settled myself to listen. "Monsieur," said she, "when the Emperor sent some Spanish prisoners here—prisoners of war or others—I had one to lodge at the expense of the Government, a young Spaniard sent to Vendôme on parole. In spite of his parole, he had to go every day to report himself to the sub-prefect. He was a Spanish grandee—excuse me a minute—he bore a name ending in 'os' and 'dia.' I think it was Bagos de Feredia, but I wrote it down in my register; if you would like to, you can read it. Ah! he was a handsome young man for a Spaniard, who are all ugly—so they say. He couldn't have been more than five feet two or three inches, but he was well made. He had the smallest hands!—which he took such care of—you should have seen—he had as many brushes for his hands as a woman has for the whole of her toilet. He had long black hair, gleaming eyes, rather an olive complexion—but I admired that. He wore the finest linen I ever saw on any one—and I have had princesses to lodge here, and among others le Général Bertrand,

le Duc and la Duchesse d'Abrantès, Monsieur Decazes,
and the King of Spain. He did not eat much; but one
couldn't be angry with him, he had such gentle, courteous manners.- Oh! I was very fond òf him, although
he didn't say two words in the day; and one couldn't
get the least conversation with him. If one tried to
talk to him, he didn't answer. It was a fad—a mania;
they're all like it, so I'm told. He read his breviary
like a priest; he went regularly to mass and to. all the
offices; and where do you think he knelt?—(we noticed
this afterward)—why, not two steps from Madame de
Merret's chapel. As he took his seat there ever since
the first time he went into the church, no one imagined
there could be anything in it; besides, the poor young
man never raised his nose out of his book of prayers.
Then, Monsieur, in the evening he used to walk on the
hill in the ruins of the castle. It was his only amuse-
ment, poor man; it must have reminded him of his
own country—Spain is nothing but mountains, so I've
heard. From the first days of his detention he was always late at night. I was anxious, when I saw he
didn't come in until just on the stroke of midnight;
but we all got accustomed to his fancies. He took the
key of the door, and we didn't sit up for him any
longer. He lodged in the house we have in la rue des
Casernes. Then one of our stable boys told us that one
evening when he was going to wash the horses, he believed he had seen the Spanish grandee swimming like
a fish some distance off in the river. When he came
back I warned him to mind the weeds. He seemed annoyed at having been seen in the water. At last, Monsieur, one day or rather one morning, we found he
was not in his bedroom; he had not returned. After

hunting about everywhere, I saw some writing in the drawer of his table, and with it fifty of the Spanish gold pieces they call portugals, equal to about fifty thousand *francs;* and afterward in a little sealed box some diamonds, worth about ten thousand *francs.* Well, this writing said that in case he did not come back he left us the money and the diamonds, and charged us to have masses said to thank God for his escape and his safety. At that time I still had my husband with me, and he ran out to search for him. Now comes the oddest part of the story. He brought back the Spaniard's clothes, which he had found under a large stone in a sort of palisade on the bank of the river, on the chateau side, almost opposite La Grande Brétèche. My husband had got there so early that no one had seen them. When he had read the letter, he burned the clothes, and we gave out according to Count Feredia's desire that he had escaped. The sub-prefect set the whole *gendarmerie* at his heels; but, pooh! they never caught him. Lepas believed the Spaniard was drowned; but I don't, Monsieur. I believe he had something to do with that affair of Madame de Merret, seeing that Rosalie told me that the crucifix which her mistress was so fond of that she had it buried with her, was made of ebony and silver. Now, during the first days of Monsieur Feredia's stay here he had a crucifix of ebony and silver, which I never saw among his things again. Now, Monsieur, you don't really think I need have any remorse about the fifty thousand *francs?* They really are mine?"

"Certainly. Then you've never tried to question Rosalie," I said.

"Haven't I though, Monsieur; but what am I to do?

That girl! she's—a wall. She knows something, but there's no getting anything out of her."

After talking to me for a few minutes more my hostess left me, tortured by vague and gloomy thoughts. I felt a romantic curiosity, and yet a sort of religious horror, like the profound sensation which takes hold of us when we go into a church at night. Under the loftly arches we perceive through the gloom a far-off flickering light, an uncertain form glides by us, we hear the rustle of a gown or a cassock—before we know it, we have shuddered. La Grande Brétèche, with its rank weeds, its worn-out casements, its rusted ironwork, its deserted chambers, its closed portals, rose up suddenly, fantastically before me. I would try to penetrate into this mysterious dwelling, by seeking for the knot of its solemn history, the drama that had slain three human beings. Rosalie was now the most interesting person to me in Vendôme. In spite of the glow of health which beamed from her chubby face, I discovered, after close scrutiny, the trace of hidden thoughts. She held within her the elements either of hope or remorse; her behavior suggested a secret, like those pious women who pray to excess, or a girl who has killed her child and is always hearing its last cry. Yet her attitudes were simple and awkward. There was nothing criminal in her broad, foolish smile, if only at the sight of her sturdy bust, covered with a red and blue check kerchief, and enclosed, impressed, and enlaced in a violet and white striped gown, you could not have failed to think she was innocent. "No," thought I, "I shall not leave Vendôme until I know the whole history of La Grande Brétèche. I will become Rosalie's lover, if it is absolutely necessary, to gain my end." "Rosalie," said I one day. "Yes! if you please, Monsieur." "You are not married?" She gave a little start. "Oh, I shan't want for men, I can tell you, Monsieur, when the whim takes me to make a fool of myself," said she, laughing.

She quickly recovered from her inward emotion, for every woman, from a fine lady to a tavern drudge inclusive, has a *sang froid* especially her own.

"You are fresh and attractive enough not to lack lovers! But tell me, Rosalie, how was it you took a place at an inn after you had been with Madame de Merret? Didn't she leave you any pension?"

"Oh, yes, Monsieur; but my place is the best in all Vendôme."

This was one of those answers which judges and barristers call dilatory. It appeared to me, with regard to this romantic story, that Rosalie stood on the middle square of the chess board; she was at the very center both of the interest and of the truth of it; she seemed to be bound up in the knot. It was no ordinary seduction I was attempting; this girl was like the last chapter of a romance. So from this moment Rosalie became the object of my predilections. By dint of studying her, I noticed in her—as one does in all the women whom we make our chief thought—a number of good qualities. She was neat, diligent, pretty—of course that goes without saying; in fact, she was soon endowed with all the attractions which our desire attributes to women, in whatever situation they may be placed. A fortnight after the notary's visit, one evening—no, one morning; in fact, it was quite early—I said to Rosalie:

"Come, tell me all thou knowest about Madame de

Merret!" "Oh, don't ask me that, Monsieur Horace,"
she answered with terror. Her pretty face grew dark,
her bright vivid coloring faded, and her eyes lost all
their soft and innocent luster. "Well," she said, "as
you wish it, I will tell you; but whatever you do, keep
the secret!" "Done! my dear child; I will keep all
thy secrets with the integrity of a robber, which is the
loyalest that exists." "If you don't mind," said she,
"I had rather you kept them with your own." So she
arranged her kerchief, and settled herself as one does
to tell a tale, for certainly an attitude of confidence
and security is a necessity in story-telling. The best
stories are told at a not too early hour, and just as we
are now, at table. No one ever told a story well standing or fasting. But if it were necessary to reproduce
faithfully the diffuse eloquence of Rosalie, a whole
volume would scarcely be enough. Now, since the
event thus confusedly related to me bears exactly the
same relation to the notary's and Madame Lepas's
gossip, as the mean terms in arithmetical proportion
bear to the extreme, I have nothing more to do than to
tell it again in few words; so I abridge.

The bedroom which Madame de Merret occupied at
la Brétèche was situated on the ground floor. In it,
sunk in the wall, about four feet deep, was a small
closet which she used for a wardrobe. Three months
before the evening when the circumstances took place
which I am about to relate to you, Madame de Merret
was so seriously indisposed that her husband left her
to sleep alone in her room, and went himself to sleep in
a room on the first floor. On this evening, by one of
those chances impossible to foresee, he came home
from his club (where he went to read the papers and

talk politics with the country gentlemen) two hours
later than he was accustomed to. His wife thought
that he had already come in and gone to bed and was
asleep. But there had been a rather animated discussion on the subject of the invasion of France; the
game of billiards too had proved an exciting one, and
he had lost forty *francs*. This was an enormous sum
at Vendôme, where every one hoards and morals are
kept within bounds of most praiseworthy moderation;
perhaps this is the source of that true contentment
which Parisians do not appreciate. For some time
Monsieur de Merret had contented himself with in-
quiring from Rosalie whether his wife had gone to
bed, and on her always answering in the affirmative, he
went straight to his own room with that simplicity
which comes of habit and confidence. But that night,
when he came in, the fancy took him to go and tell his
ill luck to Madame de Merret, and also perhaps receive
her sympathy. Now during dinner he had observed
that Madame de Merret was very becomingly dressed;
and he remarked to himself as he came from his club
that his wife's indisposition must have passed off, and
that her convalescence had made her more beautiful
than before. You see he noticed this, as husbands do
everything, a little late in the day. At this moment
Rosalie was in the kitchen, engaged in watching the
cook and the coachman play out a difficult hand at
brisque; so instead of calling her, Monsieur de Merret
placed his lantern on the bottom step of the stairs, and
by its light directed his steps toward his wife's bedroom. His footsteps were easy to recognize as they
rang in the vaulted corridor. At the moment he
turned the handle of his wife's door, he thought he

heard the door of the closet I have mentioned shut; but when he came in Madame de Merret was alone, standing before the fireplace. Her husband in his simplicity thought to himself that it was Rosalie in the wardrobe, but yet a suspicion jangled like a chime in his ears and made him distrustful. He looked at his wife; he saw in her eyes a sort of troubled, fierce expression. "You are late to-night," said she. In her voice, before so pure and gracious, there seemed to him to have come a subtle change. He made no reply, for at that moment Rosalie came in. It was a thunderbolt to him.

He paced up and down the room, his arms folded, going from one window to the other with measured tread. "Have you had bad news, or are you in pain?" she asked timidly, while Rosalie undressed her. He kept silence. "You can go," said Madame de Merret to her lady's maid; "I will put in my curl-papers myself." She divined some evil from the very look on her husband's face, and wished to be alone with him. When Rosalie was gone—or ostensibly gone, for she waited for some minutes in the corridor—Monsieur de Merret came and sat down before his wife, and said coldly, "Madame, there is some one in your wardrobe." She looked calmly at her husband, and said simply, "No, Monsieur." This "No" wounded Monsieur de Merret to the quick; he did not believe it, and yet his wife had never seemed to him purer or holier than she looked at that moment.

He rose and went to open the closet. Madame de Merret took his hand and stopped him, looked at him with a melancholy air, and said in a voice of extreme emotion, "Remember, if you do not find any one there all will be over between us!" The incredible dignity stamped upon the figure of his wife restored him to a profound sense of esteem for her, and inspired him with one of those resolves which only need a vaster stage to become immortal. "No, Josephine," said he, "I will not go. In either case we should be parted for ever. Listen! I know all the purity of thy soul; I know that thou leadest a holy life, that thou wouldst not commit a mortal sin to save thyself death." At these words Madame de Merret looked at her husband with a wild light in her eyes. "Stop, here is thy crucifix," added the man. "Swear to me before God that there is no one there. I will trust you—I will never open that door." Madame de Merret took the crucifix and said, "I swear." "Louder," said her husband; "and repeat, 'I swear before God there is no one in that wardrobe.'" She repeated the phrase unmoved. "It is well," said Monsieur de Merret coldly.

After a moment's silence: "That's a very fine thing you have, I have not noticed it before," said he, examining the crucifix, which was of ebony and silver, and very finely carved. "I picked it up at Duvivier's; he bought it of a Spanish *religieux* last summer, when that troop of Spanish prisoners passed through Vendôme."

"Oh!" said Monsieur de Merret, and hung up the crucifix upon the nail again; then he rang the bell. Rosalie did not keep him waiting. Monsieur de Merret went quickly to meet her, drew her into the embrasure of the window which looked out on the garden, and said, in a low voice: "I know that Gorenflot wants to marry you, that it's only your poverty which prevents your setting up house, and that you have refused to marry him if he can't manage to make himself a master mason—very well! go and fetch him; tell him to come here with his trowel and his other tools. Manage so as to wake no one in his house except him, and you'll make a much finer fortune than you ever even coveted. Above all, go out of this house without chattering; if you do not——" and he frowned. Rosalie went; he called her back. "Stop, take my latch-key," said he.

"Jean!" thundered Monsieur de Merret in the corridor.

Jean, who served both as coachman and confidential servant, left his game of *brisque,* and came.

"Go, all of you, to bed," said his master, making him a sign to come up close to him; then he added, in a low voice, "When they are all asleep—asleep, mind —come down and tell me."

Monsieur de Merret, who had not lost sight of his wife all the time he was giving his orders, came back quietly to her before the fire, and proceeded to relate the events of his billiard match and their discussions at the club. When Rosalie came back, she found Monsieur and Madame de Merret talking amicably together.

The Count had recently had ceilings made to all the rooms on the ground floor, which he used for receptions. It was this circumstance that had suggested to him the plan he proceeded to carry into execution. "Monsieur, Gorenflot is here," said Rosalie in a low voice. "Let him come in," said the Picard aloud.

Madame de Merret grew a little pale when she saw the mason. "Gorenflot," said her husband, "go and get some bricks from under the coach-house, and bring enough to wall up the door of that closet; you

can use some of the plaster I have by me, for plaster-
ing the wall." Then he drew Rosalie and the workman aside, and said to them, in a low voice: "Listen,
Gorenflot, you will sleep here to-night, but to-morrow
morning you shall have a passport to go abroad to a
town which I will name. I shall send you six thous-
and *francs* for the journey. You will remain for ten
years in this town; if the place does not please you,
you can settle in another, provided only that it is in
the same country. You will pass through Paris, wait
for me there; there I will settle on you, by deed, six
thousand *francs* more, which shall be paid you on your
return, if you have fulfilled the conditions of our bargain. For this sum you must keep the most absolute
silence about what you are going to do to-night. As
to you, Rosalie, I will give you ten thousand *francs,*
not to be paid over to you until the day of your marriage, and then only on condition that you marry
Gorenflot; but to marry, you must be silent; if not,
you get no dowry."

"Rosalie," said Madame de Merret, "come and do
my hair."

Her husband paced quietly from one end of the
room to the other, watching the door, the mason, and
his wife, but without displaying any offensive distrust.
Gorenflot could not help making some noise. While
the workman was unloading his bricks, and her husband was at the end of the room, Madame de Merret
seized the opportunity of saying to Rosalie: "A
thousand *francs* a year for thee, my dear child, if thou
canst tell Gorenflot to leave a chink near the bottom."
Then she said aloud, and with perfect composure, "Go
and help him!"

Monsieur and Madame de Merret remained silent
during the whole time Gorenflot took to wall up the
door. With the husband, this silence arose from calculation; he did not wish to give his wife a chance of
saying anything which might have a double meaning.
With Madame de Merret, it was prudence or pride.
When the wall had reached half the necessary height,
the cunning mason seized an opportunity when Monsieur de Merret's back was turned, and gave one of
the two panes of glass in the door a blow with his pick.
This made Madame de Merret understand that Rosalie had spoken to Gorenflot. Then they all three saw
the sad, dark face of a man, with black hair and
gleaming eyes. Before her husband had turned round,
the poor woman had time to make a sign with her
head to the stranger. By this sign she would have said
to him, "Hope!"

At four o'clock, just before daylight, the wall was
finished. The mason remained in the house, guarded
by Jean, and Monsieur de Merret went to bed in his
wife's room. The next morning, while he was getting
up, he said carelessly: "The deuce! I must go to
the mayor and get that passport." He put his hat on
his head, took three steps to the door, then turned
round and took the crucifix. His wife trembled with
delight. "He is going to Duvivier's," she thought. As
soon as he had gone out, Madame de Merret rang for
Rosalie. "The pick, the pick!" she cried in a voice of
terror; "to work! I saw how Gorenflot began yesterday; we shall have time to make a hole and stop it up
again." In the twinkling of an eye Rosalie had
brought her mistress a sort of marline, and she began
to set to work to pull down the wall with an energy of

which no words could give the least idea. She had already dislodged some of the bricks; she was gathering up her strength for a still more vigorous blow, when she saw Monsieur de Merret standing behind her. She fell on the floor in a swoon. "Lay Madame on the bed," said the Picard coldly. Foreseeing what would happen during his absence, he had laid a trap for his wife. He had really written to the mayor and sent for Duvivier. In fact the jeweller arrived just after the disorder in which the room lay had been cleared away.

"Duvivier," he asked, "did you not buy some crucifixes from those Spaniards when they passed through the town?"

"No, Monsieur."

"Thank you, I am much obliged." He darted the look of a tiger at his wife, and she returned it. "Jean," he added, "have my meals served in Madame de Merret's room, as she is very ill. I shall not leave her until she has fully recovered her health."

The cruel Picard remained for twenty days close to his wife. During the first part of the time, if any sound came from the walled-up wardrobe, and Josephine began to implore him to have mercy on the dying stranger, he prevented her from saying a single word by answering, "You swore upon the crucifix that there was no one there."

.   .   .   .   .

After this narrative all the ladies rose from the table, and the charm under which Bianchon had held them was dispelled. Nevertheless some of them had felt a sort of chill when they heard the last sentence.

THE ATHEIST'S MASS

Doctor Bianchon, a physician to whom science is indebted for a grand physiological theory, and who, though still a young man, is considered one of the celebrities of the School of Paris (itself a center of light to which all the physicians of Europe pay homage), had practiced surgery for a long time before he devoted himself to medicine. His early studies were directed by one of the greatest of French surgeons, a man who passed through the scientific world like a meteor—the celebrated Despleins. As his enemies themselves acknowledge, an intransmittable method was buried in his tomb. Like all men of genius he had no heirs; he carried—and he carried away everything with him. The fame of a surgeon is like the fame of an actor; it exists only as long as they live, and their talent is no longer appreciable after they have disappeared. Actors and surgeons, like great singers also, and those masters who increase the power of music tenfold by their execution, are all heroes of the moment. Despleins himself is a proof of this similarity between the destinies of these transitory geniuses; his name, yesterday so celebrated, is to-day almost forgotten; it will last only in his special sphere, and will not pass beyond it. But are not unheard-of

circumstances required for the name of a *savant* to
pass beyond the domain of his science into the general
history of humanity? Had Despleins that universality
of knowledge which makes a man the word, the expression of an age? Despleins possessed a divine
glance; he penetrated into the patient and his disease
by natural or acquired intuition which enabled him to
seize the diagnostics peculiar to the individual, and
taking into consideration the atmospheric conditions
and the peculiarities of the temperament, to determine
the precise time, the hour, the minute for an operation
to take place. In order thus to proceed in concert with
nature, had he studied the incessant juncture between
beings and elementary substances contained in the atmosphere or furnished by the earth for their absorp-
tion and preparation by man, in order that he may
draw from them a peculiar expression? Did he proceed by that deductive and analogical power to which
the genius of Cuvier is due?—However that may be,
he made himself the confidant of the flesh; by relying
on the present he comprehended it in the past and the
future. But did he sum up all science in his own
person as Hippocrates, Galen, and Aristotle did? Has
he led a whole school to new worlds? No. If it is impossible to deny that this perpetual observer of human
chemistry possessed the ancient science of magism—
that is to say, the knowledge of the elements in fusion,
of the causes of life, of life before life, of what from
its preparations it will be before it is, still it is but just
to admit that everything in him was personal; he was
isolated in his life by egoism, and to-day his egoism
is the suicide of his fame. Upon his tomb rises no
sonorous statue proclaiming to the future the mysteries

which genius seeks at its expense. But perhaps the talent of Despleins was part and parcel of his belief, and consequently mortal. To him the terrestrial atmosphere was a generative bag; he could see the earth like an egg in its shell, and not being able to decide whether the egg or the fowl came first, he admitted neither the shell nor the egg. He believed neither in the animal anterior nor the spirit posterior to man. Despleins was not in doubt, he affirmed. In his frank, unmixed atheism he was like so many *savants,* the best men in the world, but invincible atheists, such atheists as religious men will not acknowledge can exist. This opinion could not be otherwise in a man accustomed from early youth to dissect the being par excellence before, during, and after his life, to search him through all his organization, without finding that single soul which is so necessary to religious theories. Recognizing in man a cerebral center, a nervous center, and an aerosanguineous center, the two former supplying each other's places so well that he was convinced during the last two or three days of his life that the sense of hearing was not absolutely necessary for hearing, nor the sense of sight absolutely necessary for seeing, and that the solar plexus could replace them beyond suspicion of any change; Despleins, I say, finding two souls in man, confirmed his atheism by this fact, although it still proves nothing on the subject of God. This man, it is said, died in the final impenitence of, unhappily, so many fine geniuses; may God forgive them! The life of this really great man betrayed many pettinesses, to use the phrase of enemies anxious to diminish his reputation, but which it would be more correct to call apparent contradictions. Never having

had any cognizance of the motives on which men of
higher intellect act, the envious or stupid immediately
seize upon some superficial contradictions in order to
draw up an indictment on which they obtain a momen-
tary verdict. If, later on, success crowns the combina-
tions they have attacked, by demonstrating the relation of the preparations to the results, still a few of
their advance guard calumnies always survive. Thus
in our own time, Napoleon was condemned by his contemporaries when he stretched out the wings of his
eagle over England; 1822 was necessary to explain
1804 and the flat-bottom boats at Boulogne.

In the case of Despleins, his reputation and scientific knowledge being unassailable, his enemies found
ground for attack in his extraordinary temper and his
moral character; as a matter of fact, he certainly did
possess that quality which the English call "eccentricity." At times he dressed superbly, like Crebillon,
the tragic writer, then all at once he would affect a
strange indifference in the matter of clothes; sometimes he appeared in a carriage, sometimes on foot.
He was by turns brusque and kind, though apparently
hard and stingy; yet he was capable of offering his
fortune to his masters when they were in exile, and
they actually did him the honor of accepting it for a
few days. No man has been the object of more contradictory judgments. Although, for the sake of a
cordon noir, which physicians have no business to so-
licit, he was capable of dropping a book of Hours out
of his pocket at Court, it is certain that, inwardly, he
laughed at the whole thing. He had a profound contempt for mankind, for he had studied them from
above and below; he had caught them with their true

:xpressions in the midst of the most serious and of
he pettiest actions of life. The qualities of a great
man are often consolidate. If among these giants one
has more talent than *esprit,* still his *esprit* has a wider
range than that of a man whom one simply calls "a man
of *esprit.*" All genius presupposes intuition; this intuition may be directed to some special subject; but a man
who can see a flower must be able to see the sun. The
doctor who is asked by a courtier whose life he has
saved, "How is the Emperor?" and answers, "The
courtier is recovering, the man will follow!" is not only
a surgeon or a physician, he is also prodigiously
spirituel. Thus the close and patient observer of
humanity will justify the exorbitant pretensions of
Despleins, and will believe him—as he believed himself
—to have been as capable of making quite as great a
minister as he was a surgeon.

Among the enigmas which the life of Despleins
offer, to the eyes of his contemporaries, we have chosen
one of the most interesting, because the point comes at
the end of the story, and will answer accusations which
have been made against him. Of all the pupils that
Despleins had at his hospital, Horace Bianchon was
one of those to whom he was most warmly attached.
Before going into residence at the Hotel Dieu, Horace
Bianchon was a student of medicine, and lodged in le
quartier Latin at a wretched pension, known under the
name of La Maison Vauquer. At this place the poor
youth experienced the pangs of that acute poverty
which acts as a sort of cresset from which young men
of great talent should come forth refined and incor-
ruptible, like diamonds which can be subjected to any
shock without breaking. In the violent flames of pas-

sions, just freed from restraint, they acquire habits of
the most unswerving probity, and accustom themselves
by means of the constant labor wherewith they have
baffled and confined their appetites to those struggles
which await on genius. Horace was a straightforward
young man, incapable of double-dealing in a question
of honor, going straight to the point without palaver-
ing, and as ready to pawn his cloak for a friend as to
give him his working time or his evenings. He was
one of those friends who do not trouble themselves
about what they receive in exchange for what they
give, being certain of receiving in their turn more than
they have given. Most of his friends had that inward respect for him which unobtrusive goodness inspires, and many of them were afraid of his censure.
But Horace displayed his good qualities without prig-
gishness. He was neither a Puritan nor a preacher;
and he swore with a will when he gave advice, and
was quite ready to take his slice of good cheer if the
occasion offered. He was good company, not more
prudish than a trooper, open and straightforward—
not like a sailor—a sailor nowadays is a wily diplo-
matist—but like a fine young man who has nothing
in his life to hide, he held his head high, and walked
on with a light heart. In fact, to sum up everything
in a word, Horace was the Pylades of more than one
Orestes—creditors serving nowadays as the nearest
representation of the ancient Furies. He wore his
poverty with that gaiety which is perhaps one of the
greatest elements of courage, and, like all those who
have nothing, he contracted few debts. As sober as a
camel, and as watchful as a stag, his ideas and his conduct were equally unwavering. The happiness of

Bianchon's life began on the day on which the famous surgeon received a proof of the faults and good qualities which, the one as much as the other, made Doctor Horace Bianchon doubly precious to his friends. When the chief clinical lecturer takes a young man under his wing, that young man has, as they say, his foot in the stirrup. Despleins did not fail to take Bianchon with him as his assistant to wealthy houses, where some present almost always found its way into the pupil's purse, and where the mysteries of Parisian life were insensibly revealed to his provincial experience. He kept him in his study during consultations, and gave him employment there. Sometimes he would send him to accompany a rich patient to the baths. In fact, he nursed a practice for him. Consequently, at the end of a certain time, the despot of surgery had a *seïd*. These two men, one at the height of his celebrity and at the head of his own science, enjoying an immense fortune and an immense reputation; the other, a humble Omega, without either fortune or fame—became intimates. The great Despleins told his assistant everything. He knew if such and such a woman had sat on a chair by the master, or on the famous couch which stood in the study, and on which he slept. He knew thoroughly the great man's temperament—half lion, half bull—which at last developed and amplified his bust to such a degree as to cause his death by enlargement of the heart. He studied the strange corners of that busy life, the projects of its sordid avarice, the hopes of the politician hidden beneath the *savant;* he could foresee the deceptions which awaited the one sentiment buried in a heart not so much bronzen as bronzed.

One day Bianchon told Despleins that a poor water-
carrier of le quartier Saint Jacques had a terrible illness caused by fatigue and poverty; the poor Auvergnat had eaten nothing but potatoes during the great
winter of 1821. Despleins left all his patients; he flew,
at the risk of breaking his horse's wind, followed by
Bianchon, to the poor man's lodgings, and himself had
him carried into the private hospital founded by the
celebrated Dubois, in le faubourg Saint Denis. He
went and attended the man, and when he had cured
him gave him the necessary sum to buy a horse and
a water-cart. This Auvergnat was remarkable for an
original trait. One of his friends fell ill, so he
promptly brought him to his benefactor, saying, "I
could not bear for him to go to any one else."

Despleins, crabbed as he was, grasped the water-
carrier's hand, and said, "Bring them all to me." Then
he got this son of Le Cantal taken in at the Hotel Dieu
and took the greatest care of him while he was there.
Bianchon had already several times noticed in his chief
a predilection for Auvergnats, and especially for
water-carriers; but as Despleins made his duties at
the Hotel Dieu a sort of point of honor, he did not see
anything so very strange in it. One day as Bianchon
was crossing la place Saint Sulpice, he caught sight
of his master going into the church. Despleins, who
at that time never went a step out of his *cabriolet,* was
on foot, and slipped out of la rue du Petit Lion as if
he had been into a house of doubtful reputation. Naturally seized with curiosity, the assistant, who knew
his master's opinions, and was *un cabaniste en dyable*
(with a *y*, which seems in Rabelais to imply superiority
in *devylrie*), slipped also into Saint Sulpice. He was

not a little astonished at seeing the great Despleins—
that atheist without pity for the angels, because they
offer no resistance to the bistoury, and cannot have
either fistulas or gastritis;—in fact, the dauntless
désireur kneeling humbly on his knees, and where? In
the chapel of the Virgin, at which he was hearing a
mass. He gave for the expenses of the ceremony, he
gave for the poor, as serious all the time as if he had
been performing an operation. "He can't be come to
throw light on questions relative to the parturition of
the Virgin," said Bianchon, whose astonishment was
boundless. "If I had seen him holding one of the tassels of the canopy of Corpus Christi, it would only
have been a joke; but at this hour, alone, without any
one to see!—it certainly is something to think about."
Bianchon did not like to appear to be spying upon the
first surgeon of the Hotel Dieu, so he went away. It
chanced that Despleins had invited him to dinner that
very day, not at his own house, but at a restaurant.
At dessert Bianchon succeeded by skilful maneuvering
in bringing the conversation round to the subject of
the mass, which he pronounced a mummery and a
farce. "It's a farce," said Despleins, "which has cost
Christianity more blood than all the battles of Napoleon, and all the leeches of Broussais! The mass is
a Papal invention, based on *Hoc est corpus,* and does
not go back further than the sixteenth century. What
torrents of blood had to be shed in order to establish
the observance of Corpus Christi! By the institution
of this feast the Court of Rome, was determined to
mark its victory in the question of the real Presence—
a schism which troubled the Church for three centuries. The Waldenses and the Albigenses refused to

accept the innovation, and the wars of le Comte de
Toulouse and the Albigenses are the conclusion of the
whole affair." In fact, Despleins revelled in giving
vent to all his atheistic caprices; he poured forth a
flood of Voltairian pleasantry, or—to be more exact
—a horrible parody of *Le Citateur*.

"Ho! ho!" said Bianchon to himself. "What has
become of my morning *dévot?*" He kept silence; he
doubted whether it was his chief that he had seen at
Saint Sulpice. Despleins would not have taken the
trouble to lie to Bianchon; they knew each other too
well; they had already exchanged thoughts on equally
serious subjects, and discussed systems *de natura
rerum,* probing or dissecting them with the knives and
scalpel of incredulity. Three months passed; Bianchon
did not follow this up, although the fact remained
stamped in his memory. One day during the year, one
of the physicians of the Hotel Dieu took Despleins by
the arm in Bianchon's presence, as if to ask him a
question.

"What were you going to do at Saint Sulpice, *mon
cher Maître?*" said he.

"I went there to see a priest who has *caries* of the
knee, whom Madame la Duchesse d'Angouleme did me
the honor to recommend to me," said Despleins.

The doctor was satisfied with this excuse—not so
Bianchon.

"Oh! he goes to see bad knees in the church, does
he? He went to hear his mass," he said to himself.
He determined to watch Despleins. He made a note
of the day and the hour when he had caught him going
into Saint Sulpice, and determined to be there the year
following at the same day and hour to see if he could

:atch him again. If he did, the regular recurrence of
iis devotion would justify a scientific investigation,
:or it would not be becoming in so great a man to
;how a direct contradiction between his thought and
iis action. The following year, at the day and hour
iamed, Bianchon, who was by this time Despleins's as-
;istant no longer, saw his friend's *cabriolet* stopping
it the corner of la rue de Tournon and la rue du Petit
Lion; from there Despleins crept jesuitically along the
walls of Saint Sulpice, and again heard his mass at the
iltar of the Virgin. It certainly was Despleins! the
:hief surgeon, the atheist *in petto,* the chance *dévot,*
The plot was thickening. The famous *savant's* persist-
ency complicated it all. When Despleins had gone out,
Bianchon went up to the sacristan who had come to
invest the chapel, and asked him whether the gentleman was a regular attendant there.

"I have been here for twenty years," said the sacristan, "and all that time Monsieur Despleins has come
four times a year to hear this mass; he founded it himself."

"A foundation by him!" said Bianchon, as he
walked away. "It's as great a mystery as the Immacu-
late Conception—a thing enough of itself to make a
doctor incredulous."

Some time passed by before Doctor Bianchon, although he was Despleins's friend, was in a position to
talk to him of this strange incident in his life. If they
met in consultation or in society, it was difficult to find
that moment of confidence and solitude when one sits
with one's feet on the fire-dogs and one's head rest-
ing on the back of an armchair, when two men tell
each other their secrets. At last, seven years later,

after the Revolution of 1830, when the people rushed
upon the Archbishop's palace, when Republican in
spiration drove them to destroy the gilded crosses tha
flashed up like lightning in this immense ocean o
houses, when disbelief side by side with seditior
stalked the streets, Bianchon caught Despleins agair
going into Saint Sulpice. The doctor followed, anc
took a place near his friend without his making him
the least sign or showing the least surprise. They
heard the votive mass together.

"Tell me, *mon cher*," said Bianchon to Despleins,
when they were outside the church, "what is the reason for this *capucinade* of yours? I have now caught
you three times going to mass—you! You must give
me a reason for this mysterious proceeding, and explain the flagrant inconsistency between your opinions
and your practice. You don't believe in God, and yet
you go to mass! My dear master, you are really bound
to answer me."

"I am like many *dévots,* men profoundly religious
in appearance, but quite as much atheists as we are,
you and I."

Then came a torrent of epigrams on certain politi-
cal personages, the best known of whom represent in
this century a second edition of Molière's *Tartuffe*.

"I did not ask for all that," said Bianchon. "I want
to know the reason for what you have just been doing
here; why did you found this mass?"

"*Ma fois, mon cher ami,*" said Despleins. "I am on
the brink of the grave, so it is as well that I should
speak to you of the beginning of my life."

At this moment Bianchon and the great man hap-
pened to be in la rue des Quatre-Vents, one of the most

horrible streets in Paris. Despleins pointed to the
sixth story of one of those houses like an obelisk, with
a side door opening into an alley, at the end of which
is a tortuous staircase lit by inside lights,—well named,
jours de souffrance. It was a greenish-colored house;
on the basement lived a furniture dealer, who seemed
to lodge a different misery on each of his floors. Despleins raised his arm with an emphatic gesture and said
to Bianchon: "I lived up there for two years!"

"I know it; d'Arthez lived there. I used to come
here almost every day when I was a youth; we used to
call it *'Le bocal aux grands hommes.'* Well?"

"The mass that I have just heard is connected with
events which took place at the time when I lived in
the garret in which you tell me d'Arthez used to live;
the one with the window where the line with the
clothes on it is floating over the pot of flowers. I had
such a rough start, my dear Bianchon, that I can dispute the palm of the sufferings of Paris with any one.
I have endured everything: hunger, thirst, want of
money, of clothes, of boots and shoes, and of linen—
all the hardest phases of poverty. I have blown on my
numbed fingers in that *'bocal aux grands hommes'*—I
should like to go with you and see it again. I worked
through one winter when I could see my head steam-
ing and a cloud of my own breath rising as you see
the breath of horses on a frosty day. I do not know
where a man gets his support from to enable him to
offer any resistance to such a life. I was alone, without help, without a *sou* either to buy books or to pay the
expenses of my medical education. Not having a
friend, my irritable, gloomy, restless temperament
stood in my way. No one was willing to see in my

irritability the labors and difficulties of a man who, from the bottom of the social state where he is, is toiling to reach the surface. But—I can say this to you; before you I have no need of disguise—I had that foundation of noble sentiments and vivid sensibility which will always be the appanage of men who are strong enough to climb to any summit whatever, after having trudged for a long time through the sloughs of poverty. I could get nothing from my family, nor my home, beyond the meager allowance they made me. At this time then, all I had to eat in the morning was a little loaf which the baker in la rue du Petit Lion sold me cheaper, because it had been baked the evening before, or the evening before that. This I crumbled into some milk; so my morning meal only cost me two *sous*. I only dined every other day, at a *pension* where the dinner cost sixteen *sous*. In this way I only spent nine *sous* a day. You know as well as I do what care I had to take of my clothes, and my boots and shoes! I don't know whether we feel later as much trouble over the treason of a comrade as we feel—you have felt it too—at the sight of a mocking grin of a shoe that is coming unsewed, or at the sound of a split in the lining of an overcoat. I drank nothing but water. I had the greatest respect for the *cafés*. Zoppi seemed to me a sort of Promised Land where the Luculli of the *pays latin* alone had rights of presence. Should I ever be able, I said to myself sometimes, to take a cup of coffee and cream there, and play a game of dominoes? Well, I carried into my work the fever with which my poverty inspired me. I tried to acquire positive details of knowledge, that I might possess an immense personal value, and so deserve the place I was to reach

on the day when I passed out of my state of nothing-
ness. I consumed more oil than bread; the light that
lit me during those stubborn nights cost me more than
my food. The struggle was long, obstinate, and without any consolation. I awoke no sympathy about me.
In order to make friends, a young man must mix with
his fellows, possess a few *sous* to be able to go and
drink with them, and go with them everywhere where
students do go! I had nothing! and no one in Paris
realizes what a nothing 'nothing' is. If ever there was
an occasion which might betray my poverty, I experienced that nervous contraction of the gullet which
makes a patient believe that a ball is rising up into the
larynx out of the œsophagus. Later on I met those
people who were born rich, who have never wanted for
anything, and do not know the problem of this rule of
three: "A young man is to crime as a hundred *sou*
piece is to X.' These gilded idiots say to me: 'Then
why did you get into debt? Why did you contract such
onerous obligations?' They remind me of the princess
who, knowing that the people were starving for bread,
said: 'Why don't they buy *brioches?*' I should very
much like to see one of these rich people, who com-
plain that I charge them too much for operating—yes,
I should like to see him alone in Paris without a *sou* or
a scrap of baggage, without a friend and without
credit, forced to work with his five fingers to live.
What would he do? Where would he go to stay his
hunger? Bianchon, if you have seen me sometimes
hard and bitter, it was that I was laying my former
troubles upon the callousness and egoism of which I
have had thousands of proofs in high quarters; or I
may have been thinking of the obstacles that hate and

envy and jealousy and calumny have raised between
me and success. At Paris, as soon as certain people
see you ready to put your foot in the stirrup, some of
them catch you by your coat tail; others loose the
buckle of the girth so that you may fall and break your
head; another takes the shoes off your horse; another
steals your whip; the least treacherous is the one you
can see coming up to shoot you, with the muzzle of his
pistol close to you. You have enough talent, *mon cher*
enfant, to know very soon the horrible, incessant warfare that mediocrity wages against a man of greater
power. If you lose twenty-five *louis* one evening, the
next morning you will be accused of being a gambler,
and your best friends will say that the night before
you lost twenty-five thousand *francs*. If your head is
bad, you will pass for a lunatic. If you feel irritable,
you will be unbearable. If, in order to resist this army
of pigmies, you collect your superior forces, your best
friends will cry out that you want to eat up everything,
that you think you have a right to domineer and play
the tyrant. In short, your good qualities will become
faults, your faults will become vices, and your vices
will be crimes. If you have saved a man, you will have
killed him; if your patient recovers, it will be certain
that you have assured the present at the expense of the
future; if he is not dead, he will die. Stumble, and you
will have fallen. Invent whatever you will, claim your
just rights, you will be a sharp man, a man difficult to
deal with, a man who won't let young men get on. So
you see, *mon cher,* if I do not believe in God, much less
do I believe in man. You recognize in me, don't
you? an entirely different Despleins from the Despleins
whom every one abuses. But don't let us stir up the

mud! Well, I lived in that house; I was hard at work so as to be able to pass my first examination; I hadn't got a stiver. I had come to one of those last extremities when, you know, a man says, 'I must enlist.' I had one hope. I was expecting a trunk full of linen from my home—a present from one of those old aunts who, knowing nothing about Paris, thinks of one's shirts, under the idea that with thirty *francs* a month their nephew lives on ortolans. The trunk arrived while I was at the school; the carriage cost forty *francs*. The porter, a German shoemaker, who lodged in a loft, had paid the money and kept the trunk. I went for a walk in la rue des Fosses Saint Germain des Prés, and in la rue de l'Ecole de Medecin, but I could not invent a stratagem which would deliver me up my trunk, without my being obliged to give the forty *francs*, which I should naturally have paid after having sold the linen. My stupidity in this taught me that I had no other vocation than surgery. Delicate minds which exercise their power in a lofty sphere are wanting in that spirit of intrigue which is so fertile in resource and combination; their talent is chance; they do not seek—they find. Well, at night I returned. My neighbor, a water-carrier, named Bourgeat, a man from Saint Flour, was going in at the same moment. We knew each other in the way that two lodgers get to know each other who have rooms on the same landing and hear each other sleeping, coughing, and dressing, until at last they get used to one another. My neighbor informed me that the landlord, whom I owed for three terms, had turned me out; I had to pack off on the following day. He himself had notice to quit on account of his trade. The night I spent was the

most miserable in my life. Where was I to get a messenger to carry my few belongings and my books?
How was I to pay a messenger and the carter? Where
was I to go to? I asked myself these unanswerable
questions again and again, through my tears, like
madmen repeating their refrains. I fell asleep. Poverty has a divine sleep of its own, full of beautiful
dreams. The next morning, while I was eating my
bowl of bread crumbled into milk, Bourgeat comes in
and says in his bad French:

"'Monchieur l'Etudiant, I'm a poor fellow, a found-
ling from the hospital at Chian Flour; I've no father
or mother, and I've never been rich enough to marry.
You've not a lot of people belonging to you neither;
you've not got anything to speak of. Look here, I've
got a hand-cart down below which I've hired for two
sous an hour. It'll hold all our things; if you're agreeable, we'll look out for a place where we can lodge together, as we're driven out of this. After all it's not
such a paradise on earth.'

"'I know that, my good Bourgeat,' I said; 'but I am
in great difficulties. Down below I have got a trunk
containing linen with a hundred écus; with that I
should be able to pay the landlord and also what I owe
the porter, but I haven't got a hundred sous.'

"'H'm! I've got some chink,' he answered cheer-
fully, showing me a filthy old leather purse. 'You'd
better keep your linen.'

"Bourgeat paid for my three terms and his own, and
settled with the porter. Then he put our furniture and
my linen onto his barrow and pushed it through the
streets, stopping before every house where there was
a placard hung out. I went up to see if the place to

let would be likely to suit us. At midday we were still wandering about le quartier Latin without having found anything. The price was a great obstacle. Bourgeat proposed that we should dine at a wine shop; we left our barrow at the door.

"Toward evening I discovered in la cour de Bohan, passage du Commerce, two rooms separated by a staircase, at the top of a house, under the tiles. We could have lodgings for sixty *francs* a year each. Here then we settled down, I and my humble friend. We dined together. Bourgeat, who earned about fifty *sous* a day, possessed about a hundred *écus*. He would soon have been able to realize his ambition and buy a horse and water-cart. When he discovered my situation, for he could draw out my secrets with a depth of cunning and a kindness the memory of which even now touches my heart, he gave up for some time the ambition of his whole life. Bourgeat had worked in the streets since he was twenty-two; he sacrificed his hundred *écus* to my future."

Here Despleins pressed Bianchon's arm.

"He gave me the necessary money for my examinations. He understood, *mon ami,* that I had a mission—that the needs of my intelligence exceeded his own. He took charge of me; he called me his *petit;* he lent me the money necessary for my purchases of books; sometimes he would come in very quietly to watch me at work; in short, he took all the care of me that a mother would that I might be able to have wholesome nourishment instead of the bad and insufficient food to which I had been condemned.

"Bourgeat was a man of about forty, with the face of a medieval burgher, a prominent forehead, and a head that a painter might have taken as a model for Lycurgus. The poor man felt his heart big with dormant affection; he had never been loved except by a poodle, which had died a short time before. He was always talking to me about it, and used to ask me if I thought that the Church would consent to say masses for the repose of its soul. He said his dog was a true Christian; it had accompanied him to church for twelve years without ever having barked. It listened to the organ without opening its mouth, sitting quietly by him with an air which made him believe that it was praying with him. This man centered all his affections on me; he accepted me as a being who came in trouble; he became the most attentive of mothers to me, the most delicate of benefactors—in short, the ideal of that virtue which delights in its own work. If I met him in the streets he cast on me a look of intelligence full of inconceivable nobleness. On these occasions he walked as if he were carrying nothing; it seemed to make him happy to see me in good health and well clad. In fact, his was the devotion of the people, the love of the *grisette,* carried into a higher sphere. He did my commissions, woke me at night at certain hours, cleaned my lamp, and polished our landing; he was as good a servant as he was a father, as neat as an English girl. He kept house; like Philopœmen, he sawed up our wood; doing everything in a simple way of his own without ever compromising his dignity, for he seemed to feel that the end he had in view could ennoble whatever he did. When I left this good man to enter at the Hotel Dieu as a resident, I cannot describe the sadness and gloom he felt at the thought that he could no longer live with me; but he consoled himself with the prospect of saving up the money necessary for the expenses of my thesis, and made me promise to come on the days when we had leave, to see him. He was proud of me; he loved me for my own sake, and for his own too. If you were to look up my thesis, you would see that it was dedicated to him. During the last year of my term of residence I had earned enough money to repay the noble Auvergnat all I owed him, by buying him a horse and water-cart. He was furiously angry to think that I was depriving myself of the money, and yet enchanted at seeing his wishes realized; he laughed and scolded me together, looking at the horse and water-cart, and saying, as he wiped away a tear, 'It's too bad. Oh! what a splendid cart! you ought not to have done it. . . . The horse is as strong as an Auvergnat.' I never saw anything more touching than this scene. Bourgeat absolutely insisted on buying me the case of instruments mounted in silver which you have seen in my study; to me it is the most precious thing I possess. Although elated at my first success, he never let the least word escape him or the least sign that implied: 'This man is due to me.' And yet without him poverty would have killed me. The poor man was killing himself for me; he had eaten nothing but bread rubbed with garlic, so that I might have enough coffee for my vigils. He fell ill. As you may imagine, I spent the nights at his bedside; I pulled him through the first time, but he had a relapse two years afterward, and in spite of the most devoted care, in spite of the greatest efforts of science, he had to give in. No king was ever nursed as he was. Yes, Bianchon, I tried things unheard of before to snatch that life from death. I would have made him live, as much as anything that he might witness his own work, that I might realize all his prayers for him, that I might satisfy the only feeling of gratitude that has ever filled my heart and extinguish a fire which burns me even now.

"Bourgeat," continued Despleins, who was visibly moved, after a pause, "my second father, died in my arms. He left me everything he possessed by a will he had had made by a scrivener, dated the year when we went to lodge in la cour de Rohan. He had all the faith of a charcoal burner; he loved the Blessed Virgin as he would have loved his wife. Though he was an ardent Catholic, he had never said a word to me about my irreligion. He besought me, when he was in danger, to spare no pains that he might have the assistance of the Church. I had a mass said for him every day. He would often express to me during the night fears as to his future; he was afraid that he had not lived a holy enough life. Poor man! he toiled from morning till night. To whom else could Paradise, if there is a Paradise, belong? He received the sacraments like the saint he was, and his death was worthy of his life. No one followed his funeral except me. When I had placed my only benefactor in the earth, I pondered how I could perform my obligations to him. I remembered that he had no family, or friends, or wife, or children; but he believed; he had a religious conviction. Had I any right to dispute it? He had spoken to me timidly about masses said for the repose of the dead. He had not chosen to impose that duty upon me, thinking that it would be like asking for a return for his devotion. As soon as I could establish a foundation, I gave the necessary sum to Saint Sulpice for having four masses a year said there. As the only thing I could offer Bourgeat in satisfaction of his pious wishes, I go in his name, on the day on which this mass is said at the beginning of every season, and recite for him the necessary prayers. I say with the good faith of a doubter: 'My God, if there is a sphere where Thou puttest after their death those who have been perfect, think of good Bourgeat; and if there is anything for him to suffer, give me his sufferings that he may enter more quickly into what is called Paradise.' That, *mon cher*, is all that a man of my opinions can allow himself. God must be *un bon diable;* he could not be annoyed with me. I swear to you I would give my fortune for the belief of Bourgeat to enter into my brain." Bianchon, who attended Despleins in his last illness, dares not affirm now that the celebrated surgeon died an atheist. Those who believe will like to think that the humble Auvergnat will have come to open to him the door of Heaven, as he formerly opened to him the door of that earthly temple over which is written, *Aux grands hommes la patrie reconnaissante.*

THE END